Something About Alice

Devan Kelsey

Something About Alice

This book – and every book I'll ever write – is dedicated to my three beautiful children. I hope Mommy makes you proud. Thank you for being such sweet and gentle souls and showing me how to see the world with more magic.

To my besties, you know who you are. There are no words that I could use to express my gratitude. You celebrated every win, held my hand through every trial, and lifted my chin during every defeat. I could not have made it this far without your constant encouragement and feedback. Thank you for loving me.

And to that little girl who wrote poems in her attic bedroom with a dream...

We did it.

For permissions or inquiries, contact:
Devan Kelsey
devkelsey.author@gmail.com

Printed in the United States of America

ISBN: 979-8-218-70493-3

ONE

Why do people always leave things on the wrong shelf? Like this jar of Alfredo sauce, abandoned next to corn flakes. Because obviously that makes sense.

My feet already feel like bricks. But sure, let's carry this back to the pasta aisle like I'm some grocery store bloodhound.

Welcome to Miller's Market, where my lifelong dream of shelf-stocking mediocrity has truly taken flight. I mean, who doesn't dream of rotating soup cans and alphabetizing rice bags? Every girl's fantasy, right?

The store's unusually quiet this afternoon. I'm not about to jinx it by saying that out loud, though. Every time I do, it's like I summon an army of moms with full carts and expired coupons. Dark magic.

As I round the endcap, I hear two older men laughing in the next aisle, something about their wives sending them to "grab a few things." Their voices echo through the near-empty store. I finally find the Alfredo sauce's home, place the jar with its friends, and stand up just in time to be ambushed by perfume.

That familiar floral smell always hits *before* she does.

"ALICE! You're so hard to find!" The voice of my co-worker Christina Marwood, also known as Chris, ricochets off the shelves.

I don't flinch, but I want to.

Chris is short, curvy, and has this relentless sunshine energy that seems unnatural in fluorescent lighting. Her hazel eyes sparkle like they know something you don't. Dirty blonde hair like some well-known actress. People always say we're opposites.

Then there's me; brunette, brown eyes, plain nails and an average height and build.

I guess what they say is true, opposites attract.

I smile, because with Chris, you don't have a choice.

"Hey," I say, lifting the jar in my hand. "Just playing a thrilling game of hide-and-seek with misplaced groceries again."

She laughs like I told the best joke all day. "Wait—is that Alfredo again? I swear I've seen you put that same sauce back three times this week. Is it always the same brand?! That's *so* creepy."

How does she even notice that?

I just disassociate and do my job. Meanwhile, she's out here taking inventory of pasta sauce patterns.

I try to brush it off. "Maybe someone just has a vendetta against this brand."

Chris's eyes light up. "We should mark it. See if it's the same one getting moved around!"

Before I can stop her, she pulls a Sharpie from her deli apron. She lifts the jar, and I catch a glimpse of her nails… yellow this time, but soft, pastel yellow. Subdued. *Huh.* Usually, she's full neon and glitter bombs. Maybe she actually took my advice for once.

"There." She caps the marker. "Smiley face, bottom of the jar. If this thing moves again, we'll know."

I stare at her. "Chris… you're the sauce psycho."

She gasps. "Excuse me! I'm solving a mystery. Don't be a Debbie Downer. This place is *boring*, Alice. I'm just making it more interesting."

She's not wrong. I probably just enjoy being horizontal in bed with a book more than I do vertical with strangers in a grocery store.

"Sooo," she says, hopping beside me, "you're coming with me to that new romance that comes out this weekend, right? My treat!"

"Chris—"

"Don't 'Chris' me! You never leave your house. I'm starting to think you're part vampire. When's the last time you breathed actual air?"

"My coffin air is perfectly fine, thank you very much. I just started a new book, and I'd like to rot in peace."

"It's *one* movie," she pleads, hands clasped dramatically. "And I'll buy the popcorn!"

I sigh. I can already picture her knocking on my door if I say no. "Fine. Text me the details."

"YAY!" She bounces like she just won the lottery. "I'll get us seats. It's going to be *so* fun!"

***

A few hours later, I'm finally clocking out. My feet ache. My patience is thin. And my brain is already halfway curled up with that book I never get enough time for.

Paul, my manager, stops me on the way to the break room. "Hey, what's with Christina today? It's like a Disney overdose."

I chuckle. "I agreed to see that romance flick she's obsessed with."

He fake gags. "Knew it. She's been floating around here like a Hallmark angel."

"She wore me down with those puppy dog eyes and the cartoon-level guilt trip."

He smirks. "She's sweet though. A little much, sure. But she'd probably walk through fire for you."

"Yeah… that's kind of what scares me."

Paul laughs and waves me off.

I head into the break room, grab my stuff, and double back to the deli to tell Chris goodbye. She insists on "daily closure," or I'll hear about it tomorrow.

"Text me when you get home!" she calls out, blowing a kiss.

I lift my hand, half-wave, half-wince and grab a frozen meal from the freezer aisle. Chicken Alfredo. Because apparently, I'm on theme today.

As I open the freezer door, my eyes catch something wedged on the shelf next to the frozen lasagna.

It's a jar of Alfredo.

Not supposed to be there.

I pull it out, shaking my head. People are the worst. But just as I turn it over in my hand, my stomach sinks.

A black smiley face is drawn on the bottom.

The same one Chris marked.

TWO

No. Not again.

The creepy shit hasn't happened in weeks. I thought maybe, just maybe, it was over. But that stupid smiley face stares up at me like it's laughing.

I grip the jar tighter. "Chris, I need you to be honest with me. *Seriously honest.* Did you move this here to mess with me?"

She blinks, stunned. Her expression shifts fast—confusion turning to concern. She's too observant not to notice the shake in my hands or how flushed my face is.

"Alice… no. I swear. I went straight to the clock-in terminal after I left you, then came behind the counter. I haven't even taken my first break."

I don't respond. Just turn and walk, fast, toward the back of the store. Each step hits the tile like a warning shot. I'm not even sure where I'm going. Just that I need answers.

Where the *hell* is Paul?

I check the office. The back room. Nowhere. Another coworker finally tells me he left early to cover a shift at the store one town over.

Of course he did.

I pause in the break room, trying to catch my breath, but even now it feels ridiculous. I can't call him and accuse him of listening in on a private conversation, then planting a jar of sauce in the freezer like some grocery store ghost prank. It's absurd. All of it.

I push through the doors and out into the parking lot without looking back. People stare. I don't care. Chris gives me a look I can't read—part concern, part something else—but I can't stop. I feel humiliated. Panicked. Like I just lost a game I didn't know I was playing.

Maybe I'm losing it. Maybe it's just a misplaced jar. *Anyone* could've moved it.

But I've had this feeling before. Too many times.

I drive on autopilot, one hand white knuckling the wheel, the other gripping the jar I forgot to toss in the return bin.

It's always subtle. Just enough to make me second-guess myself. Like my sanity is balancing on a pin.

Almost a year now.

A jar out of place. Trash mysteriously emptied. Mail moved from my box to my doorstep.

Who does that?

I have one of those big green city-issued trash cans. It smells like death and leftovers and old coffee grounds, like it should. But once a month, I wheel it out on Tuesday morning and it's… already empty. And clean. Spotless, even.

At first, I thought maybe the city swapped cans. I checked. Still has my name written on the side from when I moved in.

No one admits to it. Just like no one admits to placing my mail neatly on the porch. I even chased down my mailman once. He looked terrified. I felt insane.

My mom says I'm paranoid. Probably not wrong. I mentioned it on one of our Thursday morning calls. She said I live on the "sketchy" side of town and should move. I told her I've got deadbolts on every door and windows you couldn't pry open with a crowbar. She told me to get a dog.

I told her if someone wants to murder me in my sleep, at least they'll have to break in first.

That didn't go over well.

She and dad moved south last year to somewhere warm for her joints. I stayed here. Locked in my own personal episode of *Unsolved Mysteries*.

***

I pull into downtown and slide into a spot in front of The Escape Room, the old bookstore on Main. The sign's half-lit and swinging in the breeze like it's seen better days. Most of the bulbs are out.

I come here a lot. Started about four months ago. Anything to get out of my head, away from the grocery store, and maybe into someone else's twisted fiction for a while.

Books help, and the guy behind the counter helps more.

Paul told me once that the store's previous owner—wife of our town's current mayor—vanished fourteen years ago. Her car was found a town over. Spotless. She was never seen again.

I probably shouldn't find that comforting… but I do.

Mystery feels better than madness.

The guy at the counter—Matthew Ward—is tall, scruffy, and way too charming for a town like this. I started coming in just to flirt. One day, he asked me out.

Now he's mine. The only person I want to see right now. He won't think I'm crazy. Or maybe he will. But he won't say it out loud.

I grab my phone and shut off the car.

Maybe I *should* see a therapist.

But not today.

Today, I just need someone who'll listen.

THREE

I watch him through the bookstore window, the way he moves like he belongs here—hands steady, expression calm. Just seeing him makes the tightness in my chest loosen, even if only for a second.

God, I don't know what I'd do without Matt. Even when I spiral, he's there. Solid. Safe. He grounds me.

His father used to be a carpenter, before becoming mayor, and raised Matt in sawdust and silence. Matt still carries that steadiness in his hands. The kind of hands that know how to hold you without breaking you.

He's all sharp edges and quiet strength—jawline made of stone, cheekbones you could cut yourself on, a nose too perfect to be real. His skin is golden and sun-kissed, and every inch of his arm is wrapped in inked stories. There's something about the contrast—his warm hazel eyes, his soft laugh, that ridiculously curly dirty blonde hair that keeps falling into his face—that makes you forget how much he's been through.

His mom vanished when he was still a kid. His dad vanished in a different way, to the bottom of a bottle. No yelling, no fists. Just blame. Absence.

Matt stayed kind anyway. Stayed whole. Bookish. Gentle. He should be bitter, but he's not. I don't understand how someone like him ended up with someone like me. I'm just a turtle hiding in a shell most days.

I open the door and the bell above me *dings*. I flinch, even though I expect it. My brain always seems to process sound as a threat first.

"There she is," Matt grins. "Wasn't expecting to see you until later."

He rounds the counter and pulls me into a hug, but I step back and launch into what happened at the store before I lose the nerve. The sauce. The Sharpie. Chris. The freezer aisle.

I'm breathless by the time I stop, waiting for him to tell me I'm not crazy. That it's fine. That *I'm* fine.

But he frowns, eyes sharp. "Alice…"

His hands settle on my shoulders, grounding me, but not in the way I want. His voice is calm, measured. Too careful.

"No one is moving Alfredo sauce across the store to mess with you. How would they even know which meal you were reaching for in the freezer?"

It lands like a slap.

I blink at him. "So… you think I imagined it?"

He softens, but the damage is already done. "No. I'm just saying—maybe someone overheard you talking to Chris and thought it'd be funny to mess with you both. A coworker. A bored customer."

So, this is what it feels like to not be believed.

It hurts more than I expected.

My throat tightens, but I manage, "It doesn't feel like a prank, Matt. It feels… *off*."

He sighs. "I love you. You know that. And I've always tried to listen when this stuff happens, but I can't keep pretending it's something bigger when all the signs point to coincidence."

I look at him—*really* look at him—and realize he's been humoring me. For months. Like my mom.

So maybe I *am* losing it.

My voice is flat. "Thanks for not sugarcoating it, I guess. I'm gonna head home and reset my brain. I'll call you later."

My eye twitches because that's not what I want to say. What I want is to scream *thanks for making me feel crazy!* But I nod instead, because I'm too tired to fight.

The bell *dings* again behind me as someone enters.

Matt steps away. "Hey, give me a sec, okay? I've gotta grab a book from the back for Mr. Stewart. He refuses to touch the ones on the shelf because they've been, quote, 'manhandled.'"

A small smile slips out. Only Matt could say something that ridiculous and still make me want to kiss him.

He disappears through the curtain, and I lean on the counter, flipping open a new children's book. Something about a lost bunny. Fitting.

When he comes back, he catches me off guard. "Do you want me to come stay with you tonight? Help you feel safer?"

I pause. "No. I'll be fine. I just need some time alone to clear my head."

That's a lie. I just don't want to hear him gently tell me again that I'm making something out of nothing. I don't want to see that look in his eyes, that careful mix of love and doubt.

"I get it," he says, nodding. "I love you. Call if you need me. I'll keep my ringer up."

"I love you too."

And I do. Even when he doesn't believe me.

Maybe especially then.

FOUR

With a quick kiss to Matt's cheek, I turn and walk out. I just want my bed.

Ding.

The bell doesn't even faze me this time. I fumble with my keys, eyes burning. The tears are back, and I swear if they spill before I'm off this street, I'll scream. The last thing I need is for Matt to run out and see me crying. If he sees tears, he'll follow me home. He'll cling to my side like he always does when I break.

And I can't take care of his comfort and mine right now.

I take a breath, holding it too long, trying to will the tears away without blinking. That familiar smell hits me before I even spot it—warm sugar, sweet espresso. I pause. My eyes sweep across the hood of my car.

There's a cup sitting right in front of me.

Off-white paper. Black lid. Black sleeve. Brew Crew colors.

My heart seizes. I know this drink. I've ordered it every Thursday morning for the last year while I talk to my mom.

I slowly reach for it, fingertips brushing the side like it might bite. I turn it and read the label aloud without meaning to. "Caramel macchiato. Extra drizzle."

I freeze.

I didn't buy this.

Ding.

I turn. Matt walks out the front door, his brow creased in concern.

"Alice? Everything okay?"

I don't answer right away. My gaze doesn't leave the cup.

"This was sitting on my car," I say finally, voice distant.

Matt glances at it, then at me. "Oh—yeah, I've done that before. Set mine down and forgot it. I'm glad you saw it before driving off. Your car would've needed a detail. Man, I wish you'd grabbed me one too, I'm wiped today."

I blink. "Matt… I didn't stop for coffee."

He squints slightly. "What do you mean?"

"I didn't order this. I didn't go to Brew Crew. I came straight here. It wasn't on my car when I parked. Someone left it here while I was inside."

His smile falters. "Are you sure? Maybe you meant to throw it away or something?"

I stare at him, throat tightening. He's not getting it. He's *not getting it*.

"No, Matt. This cup is hot. *Fresh*. It was just made. And it's exactly what I drink every single Thursday morning. My usual."

Now he looks at me carefully, trying to measure how far I'm unraveling.

"Okay… I'm following you. But babe—are you saying someone went to Brew Crew, ordered your drink, tracked your location, and left it on your car without saying a word?"

I don't answer right away.

Because when he says it like that, it *does* sound insane.

27

"Yes," I whisper. "That's what I'm saying."

He watches me for a moment longer. Then his posture softens, like he's trying not to say something he'll regret.

"You've had a really weird day, Alice. It's not impossible you stopped on the way here without thinking. Auto-pilot is real. Especially when you're upset."

God, I hate that he might be right.

My chest caves in with that realization. My memory is patchy. My adrenaline's been sky-high since I left the store. Could I have stopped? Ordered it and forgotten?

"You could be right," I admit, barely above a whisper. "I don't know anymore."

He helps me into the car, leans in with that gentle Matt smile. The one that says, *you're safe. Even if you're spinning out, I've got you.*

"I'll call you later," I say, and drive off.

***

By the time I pull into my garage, the sky is bleeding into dusk. I barely remember the drive home.

Just more proof, I guess, that maybe I did stop and get the damn coffee. Disassociation: my greatest skill.

I lock every door, double-check every window, and dump the coffee down the drain. Hot, perfect, and untouched. Too risky. Too weird. Too familiar.

I toss the cup into the trash and decide… bath time. Music on. Collagen mask on. Tea steeping.

Normal. Controlled. Safe.

I breathe easier under the hot water, for as long as I can handle it. Then I head back to the kitchen to toss my tea bag. I step on the trash can pedal, lift the lid— and freeze.

The coffee sleeve has slipped down.

There, hidden beneath it, is a small black drawing.

A smiley face.

My blood runs cold.

I knew it.

I'm not crazy.

FIVE

After everything that happened yesterday—and soaking in the tub for what should have been hours—I still didn't sleep more than thirty minutes at a time. Tossed, turned, stared at the ceiling. My body was exhausted, but my mind wouldn't shut off.

Now my eyes are bloodshot and burning. I look like a corpse that gave up halfway through reanimating. I'm going to need eye drops and some serious concealer if I plan on seeing another human today without being mistaken for an actual zombie.

Coffee, I love you. Please save me.

I don't work today, which is a small miracle. My plan is simply to just get through the day. I'll start by changing out the locks on the house. It's probably overdue anyway. After that smiley-face coffee stunt, I need peace of mind more than anything. A full night of sleep would be nice.

But first—cleaning. Which means facing the monstrous pile of laundry I've been avoiding for a week. The "shut the door and pretend it's not there" strategy has stopped working.

Tomorrow's problem has officially become today's disaster.

Music's blaring. Coffee's brewing. I'm in a sports bra, boxer shorts, ankle socks, and slippers—the holy trinity of day-off attire. I really hope the neighbors can't see me through the windows. This outfit was built for solitude and shame-free productivity.

I start with dishes. Mid-scrub, my phone lights up across the room. I shout at it from the sink.

"If that's work, LEAVE ME ALOOOONE."

I dry my hands and walk over. It's a text from Chris.

"Hey babes, goooodmorning! I hope you have an amazing day off and just know that if you need to talk about yesterday at all I am here for you! Also, don't forget about this weekend! Love you!"

Chris really is a great friend. I wish I could match her energy, but I'd need at least three more hours of sleep and an IV drip of espresso to even try.

"Thanks, Chris. I appreciate you. See you this weekend. "

I'm about to toss the phone onto the couch when Paul's name flashes across the screen.

Nope.

Not doing it. Unless he shows up and drags me out of these pajamas himself, I'm not going into work today. No chance.

He leaves a voicemail. My curiosity gets the better of me.

"Hey Alice, it's Paul. Heard you were looking for me yesterday and seemed upset. I had to cover the other store... total mess. Hope everything's okay. Just wanted to check in. Call if you need anything. Enjoy your day off!"

I blink.

Well, that was... weirdly wholesome.

Why is everyone being so nice to me? It's not like I had a complete breakdown in the middle of the store or anything. Right?

I glance at the little black ceramic cat on my kitchen windowsill.

Silently judging me.

Yeah, I need to find that therapist's number.

I power through laundry, start scrubbing counters, and throw together a grocery list. Matt's coming over for dinner and a movie tonight, and if he sees this place looking like a crime scene—or me looking like I just crawled out of a crypt—he's going to start genuinely worrying about my mental health.

Which, honestly, might be justified at this point.

Between loads, I decide to check the mail. I grab my jacket and save the world from seeing my day-off attire. On the porch next door, sweet old Hellen is rocking slowly in her white chair, flipping through a magazine.

She's the human equivalent of warm banana bread. On Thanksgiving she brought me a full plate of food when she saw I was home alone. When I run out of milk or eggs, she always has extra.

"You ready for that big rainstorm tomorrow?" she calls out. "I just got back from the market and they're nearly out of batteries! I grabbed a pack for you, just in case."

I glance at the sky, then back at her. "Hellen, you're too good to me. Thank you. I'm actually heading to the store later, if they're not all sold out, I'll grab some too. Is it supposed to be that bad?"

She nods, slowly. Her voice shakes a little more than usual today. "Apparently! The news says flooding's likely. Power outages, maybe. You know how this town floods. Just be safe, sweetheart."

I step up onto her porch and sink into the second rocking chair beside her. Something about this moment—the creak of the wood, the scent of old lady perfume and dryer sheets—settles the static in my chest.

She's probably pushing 80, but you'd never know it. Her hair is soft gray, pinned neatly. Nails always painted blush pink. Her jewelry glints in the sunlight— gold rings, delicate bracelet, the classic grandma trifecta.

And still, I'd bet money she was a wild child in her day.

She glances over at me. "You doing okay?"

"I think so," I say. "Just trying to catch up on life and pretend I have it together. The usual."

She smiles, knowing better than to press. "Well, I've got extra canned goods and a gas lantern if you need either. My door's always open, Alice."

Her words settle into me like a warm blanket. If I had to pick one person in this town to call family, it'd be her.

"Thank you, Hellen. I'll check the weather and grab what I need. If I miss something, I know where to come knocking."

She pats my wrist gently, her hand soft and cool. "You always have a second home here."

I squeeze her hand, kiss her cheek, and stand. "Be safe tomorrow, okay?"

She gives my shoulders a little grandma squeeze. "You too, sweetheart."

I head home, finally feeling like I can breathe again.

There's laundry to finish. Dinner to prep. And maybe—just maybe—a night that won't end with a new psychological horror.

But I won't hold my breath.

SIX

The lock clicks behind me as I step into the house, my arms full of new hardware and a plastic bag crinkling at my side. I got the replacement locks for the front and back doors, and one for my bedroom too, just in case. That one was probably more symbolic than anything else. A security blanket for my peace of mind.

I also managed to snag the last pack of batteries, plus a package of Hellen's favorite cookies. I stop by her porch and hand them off, assuring her that I have plenty of food and power essentials for the storm coming tomorrow.

She takes the cookies with a soft smile, but something flickers behind her eyes. Like maybe she wants to say something else. Warn me about something. But instead, she just pats my hand and says to let her know if I need anything.

Back inside, I pull out my phone and check the weather for the first time all day.

"Holy shit," I mutter. A massive orange and red blob is making its way directly toward our town, and it's not playing around. The forecast says it'll hit around two tomorrow afternoon and linger into the next morning. Looks like the store will be closing early. Silver linings, I guess.

While there's still daylight, I decide to climb up and clean out the gutters. The last thing I need is to wake up to flooding, or water pouring over the edge of the roof like it did last year.

The plan is to let Matt handle the locks. I may be able to climb a ladder and scoop leaves and the occasional rotting pinecone out of the gutters, but I'll be damned if I'm the one botching a lock installation. That's all him.

I've just started rinsing my gloves off on the front step when I spot Matt's beat-up red truck rolling down the street.

Perfect timing.

He pulls into the drive and is out of the truck in seconds, walking toward me with that focused kind of urgency I've come to associate with him. Not panic. Just intention.

He reaches me and without a word, pulls me in by the waist, his arms tight, grounding. My forehead rests briefly against his shoulder. Then he gently tilts my face toward his.

"I'm so sorry," he says quietly.

I pull back slightly, trying to read him. "Sorry? For what?"

His eyes search mine.

"Yesterday," he says. "You needed me, and I wasn't there like I should've been."

There it is. And yeah—he's right.

"We should talk about it after you're finished out here," he adds. "Need a hand?"

I wipe my hands on my jeans. "Actually, I'm done. But I do need your help with something else before it gets dark."

"Name it."

I hesitate. "I… picked up some new locks. For the doors. And one for my room."

His eyes soften, the corners pulling slightly down.

"Did something else happen?"

"No. Nothing specific. I'm just tired of lying awake at night listening to every creak in the floorboards and wondering if I locked the door tight enough. I know it's probably irrational, but—"

"It's not irrational," he says. "If it helps you sleep, it's worth doing. Where are they?"

That's why I love him. Even when he doesn't fully get it—he doesn't dismiss it. I lead him inside and show him where I've set the boxes on the kitchen table.

He picks one up and nods. "Let's get to work."

And just like that, I breathe a little easier.

***

Jazz drifts softly through the house as I stand at the stove, stirring pasta in the skillet. Creamy Cajun sauce bubbles and hisses, and the smell is good enough to make me weak. I pour two glasses of red wine and carry them upstairs where Matt's working on the last lock.

"Delivery," I say, stepping into the doorway and holding out a glass.

He grins and sets his screwdriver aside. "Ah, part one of my payment."

"Part one?" I raise a brow. "You're getting dinner too. What more could you want?"

He shrugs. "A shoulder massage. Maybe some undivided attention later."

I roll my eyes and sit on the edge of the bed. "You're such a diva."

But God, I missed this version of him—the one who teases and smiles and makes me feel like the world isn't collapsing.

A timer goes off downstairs, and I leap to my feet.

"Oh no! The rolls!" I dart out of the room.

Downstairs, I get everything plated just in time for him to come down and join me. I gesture to the table, and he slides into a chair like it's been calling his name.

"Wow," he says, inhaling deeply. "Alice, this smells incredible."

"I've been dying to try this recipe for weeks."

A lie. I found it online this morning. But he doesn't need to know that.

He lifts a forkful to his mouth and closes his eyes dramatically. "Marry me."

I laugh, the sound echoing through the kitchen. Finally, the air feels light.

SEVEN

Dinner was incredible.

We ate more than we should have, talked about everything and nothing, and laughed until our eyes were blurry with tears. Nights like this are why I'm so grateful for Matt. He didn't come in demanding explanations or dissecting yesterday's drama. He just… gave me space to breathe. To feel normal again. And he somehow knew I needed that without me having to ask.

We're at the sink now, shoulder to shoulder, clearing the table and loading the dishwasher together. I catch him watching me when he thinks I'm not paying attention.

"Hey, Alice," he says, drying his hands. "Hold up a minute."

Oh no. Here it comes.

I laugh, hoping it lands light enough to deflect. "What's up? Was the pasta not as good as I thought, or are you reeling over the lock situation?"

His face is serious, but there's a softness in his eyes. "Are you kidding me? That pasta was restaurant-level. I'd pay for that meal twice." He shifts slightly, leaning against the counter. "And the locks didn't freak me out. If you told me pouring pudding in your front yard would help you sleep better at night, I'd do it. No questions asked. I'd do anything for you, Alice. You know that, right?"

My chest tightens. I don't know if it's the wine or just how much I love this man, but I swear I feel tears rise and sting behind my eyes.

"I needed to hear that," I whisper. "Thank you. What do you want to talk about?"

"Yesterday," he says, his voice quieter now.

I let out a breath, leaning back against the counter. "Matt, you don't have to apologize again. I walked into your workplace in a panic over a jar of Alfredo sauce and a coffee I *probably* left on my car. You had every right to think I was losing it."

That's a lie. A total lie. Especially after what I saw on that cup. But I'm not ready to tell him that yet.

He shakes his head. "It's not about the coffee, Alice. It's your face. You were terrified. You looked like you'd been stripped bare in front of the world. Most people would've run straight to the cops. And I—I should've shown up for you better. I should've been your safe place."

And just like that, I fall in love with him all over again.

He exhales and glances away. "Yesterday wass hard for me, too. It was the anniversary of my mom's disappearance."

The air leaves my lungs. "Oh my god… Matt, I'm so sorry. I forgot. I can't believe I forgot."

He shrugs, but I can tell it hurts. "We haven't been together long enough for you to keep track of that kind of thing. It's okay. I usually take the day off work, stay home, and avoid the store. Thought maybe this year I could handle it. But when you came in, upset and overwhelmed… I guess it just hit harder than I expected."

"I should have remembered," I say. "I knew the date. You told me. I even read it in the articles. I'm so sorry."

He reaches for me, pulling me into him like he's afraid I'll float away. We stand there in the kitchen, arms wrapped tight around each other, settling quietly into the silence. He's so good. So endlessly good.

When he lifts my chin to kiss me, it's soft and steady, and something inside me unknots. Then, without a word, he sweeps me up in his arms and carries me upstairs.

So much for that movie.

Later, we're curled up beneath the sheets, his breath slow and steady beside me. My fingers trail absently along the edge of his chest when he murmurs, "Oh—your new key. I set it on your nightstand."

"My hero," I say, kissing his shoulder. "Wait… wasn't there supposed to be two?"

"Yeah," he says, sitting up. "I must've dropped the spare somewhere. I'll take another look tomorrow, and if it doesn't show up, I'll make a copy."

"Sounds good. Thank you again. For everything."

I slip out of bed to pull on some comfy pajamas, heat still clinging to my skin. I'm already halfway to the door when he finishes dressing.

"I should probably head out," he says. "I've got to be up early. Dad's making me help with storm prep for the mayoral duties or whatever."

I groan dramatically. "Come on, do you have to?"

He chuckles. "It's already midnight. You need sleep, too." Then, as he buttons his shirt, "Do you need me to pick anything up tomorrow? Last chance before the downpour."

I shake my head. "Nope. Gutters are cleared, batteries are stocked, and I've got enough books to outlast the storm."

When I glance toward my bookshelf, something flickers in my gut. A few of the spines look out of order—like they've been shifted. Not in a messy way. Just… *different*.

He must've been looking through them while working on the locks, I tell myself. Still, the unease lingers.

We walk to the front door together. One last kiss— long and slow, like we're both afraid to let go. I wait until his truck disappears down the street before I lock the door, then double-check the back door, windows, and the garage.

I even check the stove, twice.

Back in my room, I lock the bedroom door behind me and exhale with relief. I grab a book, hoping it'll lull me to sleep faster than my spiraling thoughts.

The bookshelf still feels off. Something missing, maybe? I can't figure it out. I let it go. The locks are what matter.

Twenty minutes later, my eyelids start to droop. I set the book on the nightstand and turn off the lamp. The scent of Matt's woodsy shampoo still lingers on my pillow, and it soothes me deeper into the mattress.

Finally, peace.

A cool breeze brushes my cheek.

I sit straight up, my pulse jumping like a live wire. "What the hell was that?"

My bedroom shouldn't be this cold. I haven't touched the thermostat in weeks. It's been a perfect 75 degrees for days. Maybe Matt turned it on after… you know. He probably didn't want me sweating all night.

That must be it. So thoughtful.

But then—

The crisp sound of a car speeding down the street slices through the quiet.

And that's when I feel it.

Not just the breeze.

The air shift.

My eyes dart toward the wall.

My window is open.

EIGHT

Usually, I hate when it rains… but tonight is an exception. Nights like this only make sense if there's a complete torrential downpour happening right outside my window.

When I was a little girl, rain used to be my absolute favorite thing to smell and feel on my skin. As long as there wasn't any threatening weather, my mother would let me go out and play until the ground dried or the sky turned dark. I'd jump in puddles and build tall mud castles, their towers reaching as high as my chest. The worms I found were always crowned my king and queen.

Rain reminds me of a simpler, less stressful time— but it also reminds me of when I felt the most alone. I grew up with no siblings, and both my parents worked full-time jobs. They came home, sent the babysitter away, fed me dinner, and put me straight to bed. My royal worms were my only friends for a long time.

I was about nine when a small family moved into the house next door. They had twin daughters, ten years old and gorgeous. One of them, Cassie, was quiet and withdrawn. She rarely came outside to play and barely looked me in the eyes.

But the other, Bridgette, slowly became my best friend.

They lived next door for four years. We went through everything together—from me teaching her how to make royal worm castles, to our first periods, our first crushes, and the first time we were allowed to go to the mall on our own.

She helped me grow. She broke my loneliness with just a smile.

Cassie was always jealous of our friendship. I tried to include her, but it never worked. Bridgette would just roll her eyes and say, *"Stop trying. It's not worth the effort."* I never agreed. I always thought Cassie was just misunderstood.

Then, one morning at the bus stop, they weren't there.

I didn't see them at lunch either. That weird, gnawing feeling took root in my gut. And when I got home that day and saw my mom crying on the phone— I already knew. They were gone.

Their dad had snapped. A complete mental break. No one could find the girls or their mother. He admitted to everything he did but refused to say where he'd hidden the bodies.

That was a turning point in my life. My parents put me in therapy before I could even begin to process what had happened. Looking back, I'm thankful for that— but back then, all I wanted was to run. And run. And run until I found them.

My therapist didn't get more than a few words out of me per session, but I still remember some of her advice. So, it wasn't all a waste.

I get up off my pillow-top queen mattress and crack the window open just slightly after spending my day rotting away with a book. There it is… that sweet smell of a hot summer rain.

It hasn't stopped pouring since this afternoon, and it's been so heavy the power went out hours ago.

Trying to relax, I close my eyes and take a few deep breaths.

Okay, maybe it's not the rain I hate after all. Just the memories that come with it.

I get the urge to go outside and lay in my driveway, let it soak me like it used to—but I stay under the comfort of my blankets, in my second-story bedroom.

I really *should* get up and find a flashlight. I've got at least fifteen books on my TBR shelf calling my name. On the opposite side of my room, I have three large bookshelves stretching more than half the wall. They're packed… decor scattered here and there, but mostly books.

I refuse to go downstairs in the dark just to get a flashlight or candle, so I settle for lying here, listening to the rain make soft music on my roof.

It's honestly such a peaceful moment, I'm waiting for something to ruin it. Like a loud crack of thunder or one of the windows rattling.

Still, I'm glad I went out yesterday and bought those new locks. I actually slept last night—really slept—even after the whole open window incident. Maybe tonight will be the same. Maybe I'll drift off instead of lying in bed, stuck in my usual swirl of anxiety-induced insomnia.

Another deep breath… in… and out…

Nope. It's not working.

The twins creep back into my head again.

I need a distraction.

I grab my phone off the bed and click the side button. The screen lights up. Battery's at 65%. That should be enough for a little doom-scroll session and maybe a few stupid cat videos to send to Chris.

As I'm swiping past a clip of a calico cat chasing a laser up a wall, a small noise from across the room jolts me back to reality.

And just like that, I'm aware of how terrifyingly dark my room really is.

Oh God. What was that?

My pulse quickens. I reach for my lamp, forgetting for a second that the power's out. My fingers find nothing but cold plastic.

Shit.

I fumble with my phone, swiping down as fast as I can, and switch on the flashlight.

My heart pounds as the beam slices through the darkness.

Probably the wind. Or maybe a paper fell. I just cracked the window—it's not like someone's—

My bedroom door swings open.

No.

No, no, no.

I freeze.

A jolt of pure fear shoots through me, sharp and electric.

Because I see him.

Silently standing across the room.

Eyes wide.

Locked on me.

NINE

"Oh my GOD, Matthew! You scared the shit out of me!"

I cannot believe I didn't hear him come in the house. Those cat videos were funny and all, but I'm usually so aware of every noise in my home. Missing him walking through the front door has my mind spiraling.

"Why are you even here? I thought you had to work late tonight?"

"I closed the store early because of flash flooding. Then, while I was shutting everything down, the power went out. I hadn't charged my phone since last night, so it died before I could call you. I'm so sorry I scared you." He steps further into the room. "Babe... have you been up here all night?"

I nod. "Yeah... why?"

He hesitates. "I'm not trying to freak you out, but... when I got here, your front door was wide open."

My heart sinks. No. No way. I *know* I locked that door. I *always* lock the door.

"W-what? What do you mean?"

"I mean exactly that. Your front door was literally wide open. How long have you been in your room?"

He glances over his shoulder, the shift in his body language screaming protector-mode.

"The lights have been out all afternoon," I say. "So I guess I came up here just before it got dark. But I *swear* I locked the door, Matt."

His face tightens with concern, and the air in the room feels heavier.

"There's one more thing," he says gently. "And I need you to take a deep breath before I say it."

Shit.

Telling someone to breathe before bad news never works. My chest constricts even tighter, but I do as he says and force in a shallow breath, then nod for him to go on.

"There are muddy footprints. All through the house. They lead from the door… up to right outside your bedroom."

My heart skips a beat. I blink, stunned, and then slowly get out of bed.

My legs are shaking as I walk over to him, phone flashlight in hand, and shine the beam on the floor beside his feet.

He grabs my arm when he sees how unsteady I am.

The first thing I notice are Matt's old socks—torn at the toe. He's probably the only person who's ever respected my no-shoes-in-the-house rule.

Then, just next to his feet, are two wet, muddy footprints. Pressed into my clean carpet like they've been burned there. I follow the trail with my light. They wander through the hallway like someone had been meandering around *inside my house* while I was upstairs.

How did I not hear anything?

The storm must have masked every noise. Between the wind and the rain hammering the windows, I must've tuned the rest of the world out.

"Alice," Matt says, snapping me out of my thoughts. "These are *fresh*. Still wet. I want you to go in your room and lock the door. Call the cops. Don't open it until I say it's safe. Do you understand?"

There's that protective tone I love so much.

I nod, whispering, "Be careful," and then dart back into my room, locking the new bolt tight behind me.

My hands are shaking as I fumble to dial.

"9-1-1, what's your emergency?"

"Yes, hello—there's an intruder in my house."

A loud crash erupts from somewhere downstairs—like a door being torn off the hinges—and my whole body jolts. The phone shakes in my grip.

"Ma'am?" the dispatcher says. "What was that noise? Are you okay?"

"I—I heard a huge crash downstairs. I have to help Matthew! What if he's fighting someone and I'm just *sitting* up here hiding?" Panic tightens my throat. "No, this is wrong—I *have* to go help him!"

"Ma'am, please stay where you are. The police are en route. They'll be there any second—"

"I'm sorry." I hang up before she can talk me out of it.

There's no way I'm just going to *sit* here while Matt is possibly downstairs getting murdered. What kind of girlfriend would I be?

I take a deep breath, ball my hands into fists, and open the lock as quietly as I can.

The hallway is silent.

I peek out. Nothing.

The quiet is worse than noise. It's suffocating. My heart is pounding so loud I can barely hear anything else.

I creep forward, careful to avoid every creaky board. One step at a time, I inch toward the stairs. As I reach the top step, I spot a shadow moving downstairs—someone's here.

What are they doing? Where's Matt?

Before I can figure out what I'm looking at, the figure jerks its head toward me. They bolt, darting into the living room.

No time to think.

I spin around, sprint back to my room, slam the door, and lock it in one fluid motion. Then I dive into my closet and slam that door, too. It's pitch black, and I curl in on myself, trying not to make a sound.

I sit there, counting my breaths, for what feels like an eternity.

Twenty-two.

Twenty-three.

Then—footsteps.

And the faint crackle of a police radio.

A light knock.

"Miss? Are you in there? This is Officer King, with the police department. You can come on out now."

God, I hope it's really him. What if it's not? What if I open this door and walk straight into a trap?

I crack the closet door and peek out. Light floods in from under the door, nearly blinding me.

"Come on, you're safe," the officer says.

I unlock the door, my legs wobbly beneath me.

"Who did you see?" he asks as we start toward the stairs. "Did you get a look at their face?"

"No," I whisper. "It was too dark. He saw me on the stairs and ran into the living room before I could see anything."

Each step-down feels like I'm walking through wet cement.

"Listen," Officer King says, "we're going to need you to come down to the station and give a full statement. Is there someone you can stay with tonight? Anyone I can call?"

I can't even respond. My mind is spinning. Then, as my foot hits the bottom step—

I feel it.

Something warm. Thick. Wet. I look down. My foot is soaked in something. Then I smell it. Iron.

No.

Is that… is that blood? The room spins. The floor rushes up to meet me. Everything goes black.

TEN

Groggy and confused, I start to wake up to the sound of a machine beeping steadily beside me. My head is pounding, and the sterile scent of Germ-X makes my stomach churn. My eyes won't open just yet, but I can hear someone moving around the room. Maybe a nurse? Or Matt?

As my eyelids finally begin to flutter open, I try shifting my body. Everything feels sore.

"Oh, be careful, sweetie. You're okay! You're safe, and you're in the hospital." The voice is soft and kind—older, motherly. "You took a pretty bad fall and hit your head. The CT scan shows a minor concussion."

I blink up at her, grateful. Her face matches her voice—gentle and reassuring.

"Are you in any pain? Uncomfortable in any way? I can get you something to help with that," she says, noticing my wince.

I try to nod, just barely. *Yes, please. Make the pounding stop.*

"Alright, honey. I'll be right back with something for the pain. I'll bring you some fresh ice water too."

She reminds me of my mom. I wish she were my mom… but that would never happen. My parents won't come back to this town. Not now. Not after everything.

A few minutes later, she returns with two small pills and a plastic cup of water. She helps me sit up slowly so I can take them, and I close my eyes again, trying to breathe through the nausea. Matt must be somewhere in this hospital. Once I'm stable, they'll let me go see him.

"Thank you," I manage to whisper.

She smiles, then shows me how to use the remote to call her if I need anything else. As she starts toward the door to check on other patients, a man walks in behind her—badge on his chest, notepad in hand.

"Oh for Christ's sake," the nurse snaps. "She just woke up. Can't you give her a minute for the medicine to kick in? Her head's throbbing."

"I understand your concern," he says, "but I've been waiting out there long enough. I won't push her— just a few quick questions to get the ball rolling."

I definitely imagine her rolling her eyes as she walks out.

He steps toward me, flipping open his notebook. The hospital room feels cold and distant. I close my eyes for a second, trying to gather my thoughts.

"Hello, Alice. I'm Officer Mount. I know you want to rest, but we're trying to piece together what happened at your house, and time matters in these situations, okay? Just a few questions for now."

Outside, I can still hear the rain tapping gently against the window. Somehow, it calms me. I nod— ready, even if I'm not.

"You understand you fainted at the bottom of the stairs? Hit your head on the hardwood floor."

I nod again.

"Were you alone in the house at the time?"

"No," I whisper. "Matt was there."

"Matthew... your boyfriend, correct?"

"Yes."

"Has Matthew ever threatened you in the past? Ever made you feel unsafe?"

What? I quickly shake my head. If I had the strength, I'd scrunch my forehead in disbelief. Matt is the only person I've ever felt safe with.

"Did you go downstairs at any point before the police arrived?"

"I… yes." I struggle to get the words out. "I went down… when I… heard a struggle. I had to help him."

He nods slowly, jotting something down. "And did you see anyone else? Anyone besides Matthew?"

I hesitate. "I think… I saw someone go into the living room. But I only caught a glimpse."

"So just one person?"

I pause. "I don't know. It happened fast."

He glances down at his notes, then looks back up at me with a softer tone. "Okay. That helps. We'll need to get a few things from you, just to rule out any confusion—your fingerprints, and a cheek swab. Standard procedure. Is that alright?"

I nod faintly, the lump in my throat growing.

As he closes the notebook, his eyes linger on me.

"I'll be honest, Alice… we're having a little trouble figuring out what exactly happened. There was a lot of blood at the scene. More than we expected. And right now, no one's been able to locate Matthew."

My heart skips.

"What do you mean… locate him?" My voice is hoarse, rising.

"We don't know where he is," the officer says carefully. "There's no sign of him at the hospital or any of the nearby facilities. His phone was found on the floor in the living room. That's all we've got so far."

My breath catches.

"No. No, he was right there. He was hurt—he needed help. Someone… someone—"

The machine beside me beeps faster as my chest tightens, vision starting to blur.

Footsteps rush into the room. The nurse's voice is sharp and protective again.

"Alright, that's enough! Let her rest!"

ELEVEN

The next morning, the first thing I hear is the sound of book pages turning and the scent of that floral perfume.

Chris. Oh thank GOD.

Maybe I'll finally get some answers now. If there's anyone I know who would stand up to a cop and get them talking, it's definitely Chris.

I blink my eyes open and see her sitting across the room, curled up in a chair, reading a book I recognize from my shelf. Did I lend that to her? I think I did, and it brings me a tiny bit of joy to see her enjoying it.

She's wearing a yellow sundress, a brown cardigan, and her usual cute Vans. Her hair is perfectly curled, makeup flawless. I wish I knew how she always manages to look that good so effortlessly.

"Ch-Chris?" I mumble out. Ugh, my face is numb again.

"Oh! Oh my God! You're awake!" She jumps up, practically knocking the book to the floor. "Okay—I'll be right back. Let me go get the nurse!"

She's such a spazz.

"N… no wait." The words drag out of my mouth. I will never take my normal face for granted again once this is all over.

She crosses the room instead, her expression flipping from excited to concerned. "You don't want me to get the nurse? Are you uncomfortable?"

I shake my head slowly. My face is beginning to thaw.

"I need to know… what the hell is going on… and WHERE the hell Matt is. Before I passed out, a cop was here… He said there was blood and something about… not knowing Matt's location." Just saying it makes my stomach roll, and the dizziness creeps back in like a warning.

Chris bites her lip nervously. "Alice… I really think I should get the nurse first. You hit your head really hard, and they've got you on some strong meds."

She pleads, but I'm not having it.

"Fine." I sigh. "Just tell the nurse to be quick."

I can never win with her.

The nurse comes in, checks my vitals, and reminds me I can't have any more pain meds yet, but she'll come back and check on me soon.

As soon as the door clicks shut, I turn to Chris. "Alright, there you go. I'm stable enough. Talk."

She hesitates.

"Okay, so don't be mad," she starts, her voice low. "I might have, uh… accidentally overheard one of the officers. He stepped out to take a call while you were sleeping. He was pacing right outside your door. And, well… he wasn't exactly being quiet."

I lift an eyebrow. "Overheard how much?"

"Enough to know that Matt's definitely still missing. They found a lot of blood… and something about a creepy note. It matched a pad of paper from in your house."

My stomach twists like a soaked rag. "I don't understand."

"I know," she says quickly. "But that's what they're saying. And apparently… there were no other prints in the house. No forced entry. Nothing. They're not saying it out loud yet, but…"

She hesitates again.

I stare at her. "They think *I* did it?"

She doesn't answer. Her silence is answer enough.

We sit in silence for a good two minutes while I try to process everything she just told me. She just patiently waits for my brain to stop spinning. I can feel the air tightening around us.

"Wait," I finally say, my voice cracking. "Did you say that Matt is… missing? They don't know where he is? Or who took him?" My voice starts rising. "They don't know anything?! What's the point of cops if they can't even protect the people who need them?! This is *bullshit*!"

Chris flinches but doesn't try to stop me. She lets me scream it out. Years of unhealed trauma—Cassie. Bridgette. Every time I've felt powerless. It all starts bubbling up.

Chris waits until I've deflated a little before adding, "Your mom called your room while you were out. I answered and told her you were okay. Well—safe, at least. I explained the basics of the situation. She said she's flying in to stay with you for a few weeks."

Oh God. No. No, no.

"Can you call her back and tell her not to come, please? I don't need to be lectured on my life choices right now." The amount of bitterness on my tongue that came out with those words surprised us both.

"Alice," she says gently. "You might not have a choice. She *needs* to come. Matt is missing. And with the way the cops are already spinning things… it looks like you could become a suspect. You're going to need your parents' support."

She hesitates. "Your mom said your dad couldn't get away from work, go figure, but she's working on a flight here as soon as possible."

A suspect? *Me?*

No. They can't honestly think that. I was trying to help Matt. I'm the one who called 911. They have that call. They have to.

There's no possible way they think I made this up. That I did something to him. That I'm making up this whole story to play the victim.

Maybe… maybe it's time I tell them everything. The creepy things that have been happening. The notes. The smiley face. Someone's been watching me. That has to mean *something*.

I breathe slowly, trying to steady myself. The ache in my head is crawling back. I scan the room to distract myself—and then I spot it.

A vase of flowers on the windowsill.

They're gorgeous and whimsical. Wildflowers. All different kinds, colors, and shapes.

"Who sent those?" I ask. "You? Or my mom?"

Chris frowns, glancing over. "Not me." She stands to smell them. "Maybe your mom?"

"I don't think they were here earlier when the cop was questioning me," I say.

Chris starts digging around in the bouquet and lights up. "Oh! There's a note." She plucks it from the center and brings it over. "It doesn't have a name. Maybe Paul had the store send them?"

I blink, trying to adjust my vision. The handwriting is familiar. Too familiar. And the note *is* signed.

Chris just doesn't realize it.

71

Feel better soon. ☺

It's the same handwriting. The same smiley face.
I've seen it one too many times before.

Whoever this is… They've been watching me for a
long time.

TWELVE

I barely slept after that note. The handwriting was burned into my mind like a brand. When the nurse came in the next morning with my discharge papers, I didn't even argue, I just needed out.

The hospital sent me on my way with some pain meds and instructions to take it slow and not push myself too far. My head was still sore, but they said it was just a minor concussion and a surface wound from where I broke the skin hitting the floor.

Today is Thursday, and I find myself wishing it were already the weekend—so Chris could be convincing me to go to the movies, regardless of the chaos happening around us. She'd say that going for two hours would help me breathe and relax, and that there was nothing I could do but sit home and worry anyway.

She's probably right. I just want a distraction from the noise in my head. From the panic about where Matt is right now.

I'll never understand why hospitals insist on wheeling you out the front doors in a wheelchair. I hit my head—I didn't get my legs chopped off.

"This is so unnecessary," I mutter to the kind-faced nurse in scrubs. He looks sweet, but I hate people going out of their way for me, and this is pushing my limits.

When the double doors open and the sunshine hits my face, a full-body wave of relief rolls through me. Freedom. Finally free of that sterile, humming, fluorescent hell.

Only to be met by that damn cop leaning on his car like we're old friends.

"Hey, Alice. Good to see you on the outside," he chuckles.

"Where's Chris? She's supposed to be driving me home." I don't even glance at him. I have zero energy for forced friendliness. "She went to get the car."

"That actually won't be happening. I'm going to need you to come down to the station with me. You've been summoned for a formal statement. I already talked to your friend and sent her on her way."

My pulse jumps. This man is not getting me into his car without a fight.

I scan the lot. There. Chris—pacing in front of her car, phone pressed to her ear, mascara smudged. She mouths something I can't quite catch. Maybe "your mom," before we turn the corner and she vanishes from view.

"Wait—there she is. In the back of the lot. I see her car. I'm not leaving with you."

I reach for my phone to call her and get her to come save me, but before I can, his hand twitches— subtly but deliberately—as if to stop me.

"I think you're misunderstanding," he says. "This isn't optional. You're leaving with me whether you like it or not. Even if you call her and she drives over, there's nothing she can do. So let's do this the easy way. You've been through enough the past two days."

His voice is calm, and his eyes are kind. But his hand rests near the cuffs on his belt.

I hate it. I hate all of it. But I comply. Only because I refuse to be restrained like some kind of animal.

As we drive, I lean my head against the window and let the world blur past me. Trees. Sidewalks. Empty lots.

It takes me back to the days after we found out what Cassie's dad did to them. How life just… went on. We returned to school. People made casseroles. But she was still out there, lying in the woods somewhere. Lifeless.

Tears slide down my cheeks.

Cassie missed everything. Middle school dances. Graduation. First job. Drive-in movie popcorn. Falling in love.

All because her dad snapped. They blamed it on money. Said he had a gambling problem. Owed the wrong people. Got in too deep. But I don't think that's what broke him.

I wonder how he felt sitting in the back of a cop car, knowing what he'd done. Was he proud? Was he ashamed?

He was a coward. He deserved every second of what happened to him behind bars.

The car pulls into the station and jolts me back to the present. The officer steps out, walks around, and opens my door. I hesitate.

I want to run.

But I'm still dizzy, and my body betrays me—so I let him help me to my feet.

He guides me through the most depressing hall I've ever seen and into a cold, lifeless room: the interrogation room.

He pulls out the chair for me and offers water. My mouth feels like it's full of cotton, so I nod.

"It's going to take me a bit to get everything situated," he says. "Try to get comfortable. I'm grabbing a pen and a notepad. I need you to write a detailed statement. I'll be back soon."

Get comfortable? Right.

He shuts the door harder than necessary, making the window rattle.

I stare at the scuffed floor, the stain on the wall, the buzzing light overhead. This room smells like old sweat and bad coffee. I hate it here. I hate knowing someone could be watching from the other side of that glass, judging every breath I take.

How many people have sat in this exact chair before me? Drunks. Thieves. Liars. Killers.

And now *me*.

Why?

The cop—what *is* his name?—comes back, sets down the paper and pen, and places a plastic cup of water in front of me. It tastes like metal and mildew. Either a strategy to break me, or they just haven't cleaned the pipes since the '80s.

"Do I bring it out when I'm done or wait?" I ask.

"Just wait. We'll be in soon," he says. Then pauses. "And be honest. Make this easier on yourself."

Did he just wink at me? Gross.

I pick up the pen, turn the page, and begin to relive one of the worst nights of my life.

I've never disassociated this hard before.

I force my brain to pretend I'm writing fiction. That this is a story. Someone else's. Not mine. Anything to keep the memories at a safe distance.

This town may be small, but it's full of people. And people don't always make the right choices.

Maybe a few of them sat here after stealing beer. Or crashing their car drunk. Or hurting someone.

Maybe someone just like Cassie's dad sat in this chair. Someone who snapped and never came back from it.

A shiver runs through me, even though it has to be at least 85 degrees in here.

Why *am* I sitting here? What if I've been spiraling this whole time?

What if none of this happened the way I thought? What if I did something… and just don't remember?

THIRTEEN

After what feels like a decade, the cop finally comes back into the room. I still haven't bothered to learn or remember his name—because I won't be here long. I didn't do anything. They're just filling in the gaps and clearing things up.

"I'm sorry I had to bring you in straight from the hospital," he starts, trying his best to sound sympathetic, "but that was just how the timing played out. I need your memory as fresh as possible, so your imagination doesn't kick in and add anything."

He talks to me like I'm five. I nod but stay silent. I've seen enough crime shows to know better—anything I say can and will be used against me.

"Alright," a new guy walks in and says. He dismisses the other officer and settles into the chair across from me. "I'm just going to get into it."

Good. Let's get this over with.

"I'm Detective Harper," he says, flipping open a folder in front of him. "There was no sign of forced entry at your house. No signs of a break-in at all. Nothing stolen. Nothing noticeably out of place. Obviously, we don't live there, so maybe something *is* missing, but…"

He glances up at me, checking if I'm following.

I nod once. Still numb. Still waiting for this nightmare to end.

"Basically, what I'm saying is: other than the muddy footprints throughout your home, and the sound you claim to have heard from downstairs, there's no real evidence that someone entered your house, hit Matthew over the head, and kidnapped him."

He leans forward like he expects me to confess. I say nothing.

We sit in silence, tension stretching the space between us.

Then he sighs, voice softening, like he's trying to give me one last chance.

"Is there anything else you haven't told us, Alice? Something that might help us understand what's going on?"

That's when it hits me. If I don't say something now—if I don't give him *something*—they're going to write me off as the only suspect.

So I do it. I open my mouth.

"Yes," I whisper. "Actually... yeah. There's a lot."

His pen stills on the page.

"I didn't tell the officer at the hospital, mainly because I was pretty out of it but also because I didn't think anyone would believe me. It sounds... paranoid. But weird things have been happening. Quite often for weeks now but started months ago"

He narrows his eyes, waiting.

"Little things at first. My mail kept being left on my porch, not in the mailbox. I asked every neighbor I have, even chased down my mailman once, and no one did it. My trash cans, the ones issued by the city, randomly empty and clean. I don't know who does that either. Small little insignificant things to make me feel like I'm going crazy." I pause to study his face.

"Then recently, it's become a little more aggressive. There was this jar of alfredo sauce that got moved around the store I work at. My friend drew a smiley face on the bottom to see if it was the same jar, and it *was*. A coffee cup left on top of my car—my exact order. I noticed later the cup had a smiley face drawn under the sleeve. There was even a vase of flowers at the hospital with a creepy note inside with the smiley face. It's like whoever is messing with me took the smiley as their *signature*."

"What kind of note?"

I swallow. "It said, 'Feel better soon.'"

He raises an eyebrow.

"There were noises too," I go on, faster now. "In the middle of the night—like someone in the house. I kept brushing it off, but I knew something felt wrong. I kept seeing things out of the corner of my eye. The front door unlocked itself one night while I was upstairs. I know how that sounds, but I'm telling you the truth."

Harper just watches me.

"I didn't imagine any of it," I say, quieter now. "I think someone was messing with me. Watching me.

Maybe even living in the walls for all I know. And now Matt's gone. Someone *took* him. I swear to God, I didn't do this."

For a split second, his expression softens. Not much—but enough for me to see it.

A pause.

Then, calmly, Harper reaches into the folder and pulls out an evidence bag. Inside is a single folded piece of paper, partially stained dark.

He doesn't say anything—just turns the bag over so I can read what's on the back.

A smiley face. Drawn in red.

My breath catches. "What is that?"

"It was tucked behind a floorboard in your living room. One of our techs found it near the blood."

My heart thuds in my chest. "I've never seen that before."

He studies my face carefully. "We had it analyzed. The only fingerprint on it was yours."

"No," I say immediately, voice cracking. "That's not possible. I didn't touch that—I've never seen it. I didn't even know it was *there*."

He leans back slowly. "Then how do you explain that, Alice? Because unless this kidnapper wore gloves and left no trace, it looks a lot like you wrote it."

I shake my head, heart pounding. "Someone's trying to frame me. I know how that sounds, but please—you *have* to believe me."

He sets the bag down.

"We also found a bookend hidden in the bushes behind your back fence," he adds. "Only one set of prints on that too."

"Let me guess," I whisper.

He nods. "Yours."

The walls close in. My ears start ringing.

"I didn't do this, that stuff is probably from my house! How else would my fingerprints be on it?! I didn't do this!" I repeat, the panic rising. "He was *hurt.* I heard a struggle. There was blood—I tried to help. Someone was *in* the house. I heard them—"

"Whose muddy boots were by the front door, Alice?"

I blink, caught off guard. "Matt's. Why?"

"They were covered in fresh mud. The same mud tracked across your carpet. But you said Matt always takes off his shoes at the door."

"He does. He always does."

"Then explain the footprints. Because if he was knocked out and dragged away, how'd he walk through the house first?"

I don't have an answer. Not one he'll accept.

I close my eyes, trying to remember every detail. "Maybe he kicked them off in a rush. Maybe he panicked. Maybe the person who *took* him put them there to confuse you."

Harper watches me like he's measuring my unraveling.

The door swings open before I can say anything else.

A tall brunette in a gray suit steps into the room, heels clicking sharply across the floor.

"Don't say another word, Alice."

She looks calm. Controlled. And completely in charge.

Whoever she is, she's here for me.

FOURTEEN

Walking out of the station beside the woman who just saved my sanity, I spot a familiar figure pacing in front of a blue Toyota.

My own face, but aged.

Mom.

Her head snaps up at the sound of the door swinging open. She rushes over, tears streaming down her face, and pulls me into a tight embrace.

"Oh, honey! I cannot believe this is happening. I'm so glad you're alright. I tried to get here before the hospital discharged you, but I got delayed." She's a blubbering mess on my shoulder—and I'm thankful for it.

That familiar scent of her shampoo, the way she holds me, letting the stress melt from my muscles... I need her right now. We haven't always seen eye to eye, and I may not be the best daughter, but in this moment, I need my mom more than anything.

After everything that happened with Cassie's family, my relationship with my parents was never the same. My dad became a recluse, burying himself under the guilt of thinking he could've stopped what happened—thinking he could've saved them. He carried the weight of comparing himself to the man who took their lives. My relationship with him became strained, awkward. Forced. And it just didn't survive.

I don't blame him any more than I blame myself. I still love him, and I know he loves me. But we've never quite recovered.

My mom, though… her grief manifested differently. It was like she mourned my childhood before it was even over. I think she saw the trauma harden me too quickly, and it shattered her heart. She tried to keep me in pink frilly dresses, tried to hold on to my innocence with both hands while it slipped through her fingers. I understand now why she did it, but back then, it always ended in screaming matches and tears.

But now, with her arms wrapped around me, that little girl—the one who just learned her best friend was murdered by the man meant to protect her—resurfaces. My shoulders drop. My legs turn to Jell-O. I melt into her, and I *sob*.

Big, heaving, body-shaking sobs. I soak her shirt with my tears, surprised she doesn't pull away in shock.

I can't even remember the last time I cried in front of her, let alone hugged her. But she holds me tighter, grounding me, while years of trauma and what-ifs spill out onto her chest.

I needed her. And I doubted she'd show up. I feel so guilty for that.

Not only did I lose my best friend, but she lost hers too. She and Bridgette's mom used to sit out on the back porch drinking wine, watching us girls play until the sun went down. They were family. Even *he* was part of that. He borrowed tools from my dad. Helped fix our fence after a storm.

They were real people. Good people.

Sometimes, my mind won't let me remember that part. But standing here, I do. I remember the good. I remember what we lost. Not just the three of them, but *us*, too.

I pull away from my mom's embrace, drenched in tears. Face, hair, clothes—all soaked. And then it hits me again.

"They think I killed him, Mom! They think I killed Matt!"

My knees give out, and I start to drop, but her grip tightens. She pulls me back to my feet, arms steadying me.

"I know, baby. And we're going to fix this, somehow." She glances toward the woman beside us. "Claire is a damn good lawyer. The best. I hired her the second I knew you were in trouble. If it comes down to it, she'll fight tooth and nail for you. You are *not* going down for something you didn't do, do you understand me?" She lifts my face so our eyes meet. "Alice, *do you understand me?*"

"Yes." It's all I can say. Just because I understand her doesn't mean I believe a word of it.

From what that detective said, they have so-called *evidence*. Fingerprints. A bookend. That creepy note.

Things that shouldn't be adding up, but somehow, they are—against me.

My mom helps me wipe my face with some tissues from her purse, gently tucking my hair behind my ear like I'm ten years old again.

"Stand tall. Confident. Chin up. You don't let them think you feel guilty. Unless you've got something to tell me—like you killed your boyfriend and hid his body—then don't let your face slip. Got it?"

I blink at her, stunned by the bluntness, but I should've expected it. That's just who she is.

"I don't have anything to tell you," I say flatly. "Everything I'm being accused of is false. I didn't do this, Mom."

She studies me for a beat, then nods.

"Alright then. We've got work to do. Let's get you changed, get some food in you." She turns to Claire—the woman who hasn't said a word until now.

"We'll meet you at the coffee shop in an hour. That okay?"

Claire smiles politely. She's all business, but there's something warm in her tone that puts me at ease.

"Yes, ma'am. I'll head over now and get started on paperwork and research about the town. Call me if anything changes. If not, I'll see you both soon." She turns to me. "Alice, I'm going to get you through this."

Her confidence carries weight. I believe her. And for the first time in days, I feel like maybe—*maybe*—I'll be okay.

We head to my mom's rental car.

"I'm sorry your father isn't here," she says as we buckle in. "There's a huge project at work. He was ready to drop everything and come, but I told him I could handle this part. Once he's wrapped up, he'll drive in. He doesn't do well with these kinds of situations anyway. I figured it would be easier on you if he stayed back a few days. I hope that's alright."

"No, I get it. Thank you for thinking of me." I pause. "But... I can't go home yet. It's still a crime scene."

Her face pales.

"Oh god, I didn't even think of that. Okay, we'll go to the store, get you some clothes, and then grab a hotel room for a few days. Sound good?"

She's always been good at practical solutions.

"Yeah, that's fine," I say, reaching into the brown paper bag I was handed at the station. I pull out my phone, praying for a message from Matt. Something. Anything.

But there's nothing. Just texts from Chris, coworkers, and my mom—before she knew where I was.

As I'm scrolling, clearing notifications, my phone lights up.

A call.

Paul.

FIFTEEN

"Ugh! They can't give me two seconds to breathe, can they? It's like he *knew* I turned on my phone!" I huff.

"Who?!" Mom asks, confused.

"My boss—Paul. I'm really not in the mood to talk about what happened right now, but I guess I'll answer and make sure everything's alright at work. I could use the distraction." I roll my eyes and flip off my phone before swiping to answer.

"Hey, Paul. What's up?" I ask, my tone making it clear I'm not exactly thrilled to be talking.

"Oh my god, you answered! I was *not* expecting that. Someone told me you got arrested. How do you even have your phone?! Wait—no, don't answer that. That's not why I called."

"Jesus, Paul. Take a breath and tell me what you want. This isn't a good time, and no—I was not arrested!" My heart rate spikes. My knee starts bouncing hard enough to shake the whole car. Mom places a firm hand on it and shoots me a look. Breathe.

"Have you heard from Christina? Her shift started over two hours ago, and no one's seen or heard from her. She's *never* been late. Not once. And with everything that's going on with you, I'm getting really worried."

My stomach twists. The air I was holding in my lungs drains slowly out of me. My vision starts to blur, and my chest tightens, constricting more and more. I can't seem to take a full breath.

A panic attack. In front of my mom.

Fantastic.

"Alice? Are you there? Did you hear me?"

Paul sounds so concerned, but I can't form a coherent thought. All I can think about is that whoever took Matt… has taken Chris too. And what if I'm next?

"Y… yeah. I—I hear you. I… I haven't talked to her since... since I left the hospital."

My voice shakes, but my mom grabs my hand and squeezes it. I start to calm. She speaks loud enough for Paul to hear too.

"You saw her just a few hours ago," she reminds me gently. "She's probably just at home sleeping. She stayed up all night worrying about you."

Right. She *has* to be at home. She probably laid down and zonked out. That's all it is.

"Okay, well… that makes me feel a little better." Paul exhales, and I notice I breathe with him. "If you hear from her, can you let me know? Please?"

"Yeah. We'll drive by her place on our way to the store. I'll check in." I glance at Mom and she nods, already turning toward the road.

"Okay, thanks, Alice. Oh—and don't worry about work. I've got your shifts covered until next Friday at least. Talk soon."

He hangs up before I can say anything.

I turn to Mom again and she says, "Just tell me where to go."

I dig through my old texts to find Chris's address— I've never actually been to her place before. It's only about a 12-minute drive.

96

On the way, Mom calls Claire to let her know we might be a little late.

We turn onto a quiet street and slow as I spot her house number on the side of the wooden mailbox. It's a cute little two-story home, kind of like mine, but her car isn't in the driveway.

There's no sign of anyone. No movement. No lights. No Chris.

"Should I go knock?" I ask.

"Up to you," Mom replies.

I nod, get out, and walk quickly toward the front steps. My gut is churning but I tell myself she's just inside. Maybe she lent someone her car for an emergency. That sounds like something she'd do.

I pause at the door and take a steadying breath before knocking.

Nothing.

I knock again. Wait. Still nothing.

"She might be asleep. Or in the shower," I mumble to myself.

I pound harder—my knuckles reddening with each hit.

"Dammit, Chris! ANSWER THE DOOR!" I yell, desperation cracking my voice.

If she *is* home, she's probably going to be pissed at me for shouting like a lunatic outside her house. But I don't care. Not right now.

She *has* to be here. There *can't* be another explanation. She's *fine*—she has to be.

The air in my lungs gets thinner. I slowly turn away and begin stepping off the porch, barely able to keep moving.

This is when I wish therapy had helped more. I don't have the tools for this kind of emotional overload.

I feel like I'm back in middle school, back in that moment when I heard Bridgette and Cassie were gone. Cold, lifeless bodies lying somewhere out of reach.

A shiver runs down my spine. Tears prick my eyes.

"I can't lose my best friend again."

Wait—did I just say that out loud? I did. Gross.

I turn toward the street and take a deep breath, willing myself to get back to the car. Just keep walking. Left foot, right foot.

My foot hits the top wooden step with a soft creak. That's when I see it.

Something down near the sidewalk. Just a flicker of color. I squint, trying to make it out through the blur of tears and rising panic.

A small, scuffed box.

Yellow chalk.

My knees buckle.

"Mom! Get over here!" I shout. "I—I think I'm gonna pass out!"

She's at my side in an instant, gripping my arms, trying to steady me. I see the concern in her eyes, but also the confusion.

She doesn't understand.

She doesn't *see* it yet.

"What is it, Alice? What's wrong? Is she home or not?! I don't get what's happening!"

She's begging for an explanation, but I can't find the words. I can barely stand.

Then she follows my gaze. Squints. And finally sees what I see.

Her eyes widen, but her confusion deepens. She doesn't know what it means. Not really.

But I do.

Right there, drawn on the sidewalk next to that ugly little box of chalk, is a simple, haunting mark:

A yellow smiley face.

SIXTEEN

The ride to the hotel feels like a blur, and I can't even focus on the hundreds of questions my mother is throwing at me. My head leans against the window, hitting the same sore spot with every bump in the road. I'm in full dissociation mode. I don't understand how my life ended up here. Have I not been through enough already?

My boyfriend is missing. I'm being investigated for his disappearance—and possibly his murder. And now my best friend is probably gone, too.

If I know anything about that smiley face, she's definitely not down at the market, clocking in late for work.

Who is doing this to me? More importantly—why?

I don't have enemies. Not here, not anywhere. I'm quiet. I keep to myself. I know I'm not the most fun or outgoing person, but that's hardly a reason for someone to try to destroy my life.

And if I'm next? If they come to take me away too?

Honestly, let them. I'd trade places with Matt or Chris in a second. If anyone deserves this, it's me. I couldn't even protect the twins from their own father.

I should be the one they want to erase from the world.

I just need the cops to believe me. I need them to stop circling around me like I'm the one responsible and start helping me figure out where Matt is. They need evidence—real evidence—that proves I didn't do this. Whoever is setting me up has done a disturbingly good job. Every clue points back to me.

They're smart. I'll give them that.

"I hope this lawyer you hired is good at her job. If Chris is missing too, they're definitely going to try to pin this on me."

The monotone voice that escapes me doesn't even sound like mine. She sounds hollow, broken, like she's given up before the fight's even started.

No. I'm raging inside. I'm not allowed to shut down.

My heart and brain need to get on the same page because I can't mourn and go to war at the same time. That kind of inner chaos is what triggers my panic attacks.

"Alice," Mom says, "just because she wasn't home doesn't mean she's missing. Her phone could've died. Maybe she had an emergency. There are *so* many possibilities. Don't jump straight to the worst one."

She's trying to keep me grounded, but she doesn't understand. She hasn't *seen* what I've seen. That smiley face—it means Chris is gone. I can feel it in my bones.

Mom takes me to get clothes and food, but I can't stomach a single bite. I told her we needed to report Chris missing, but she insisted we wait until we talk to Claire. The whole thing feels surreal. My brain is constantly trying to escape my body. I want to go home. But I *can't* go home.

And no one seems to understand: if someone has Matt—and now possibly Chris—I'm probably next.

***

After the meeting with Claire, Mom asks if I feel any better.

I don't.

If anything, it made it worse. It made it *real*.

My boyfriend is actually *missing*. There's a *pool of his blood* on my floor, at the bottom of my staircase. And no one knows where he is. Or who took him. But everyone *does* seem to think I had something to do with it.

We have a short window to find something that clears my name before the cops bring me back in. This time I'll have Claire beside me, but I'm not sure her presence will make me feel any less like I'm drowning.

We head back to the hotel. Mom's hoping to upgrade our room—they only gave her a single bed, and she hadn't thought I wouldn't be allowed to go home. I love her, but I am *not* sharing a bed with my mother unless it's life or death. She'll try to snuggle me like I'm six again and that sounds like my personal hell.

She wants to sit down in a quiet space and pick my brain—see if I've forgotten to mention anything to the cops. Maybe something I brushed off during the initial shock of it all. I guess that makes sense, but the idea of her digging through my mental archives is not exactly appealing.

While she's sweet-talking the front desk guy—a short, nerdy-looking twenty-something with a cross tattoo that *definitely* looks like it was done in someone's basement—I carry her luggage and my bags to a nearby sitting area and sink into a musty red couch.

There's a sad little pile of magazines on the side table, next to a drink coaster, as if one more water stain would somehow ruin the ambiance.

Claire had said if I hadn't heard from Chris by tomorrow, we'd report her missing during our next meeting with the detective. The thought of her being out there—*somewhere*—while we're just sitting around waiting makes me sick.

Chris is too kindhearted for this cruel world. If someone asked her to go quietly, she would. She'd follow the rules. She'd listen. Me? I'd go down swinging.

Which is probably why I'm still here. And why she's not.

I'm angry. Angry that no one is out there looking for her. Angry at myself for not knowing more about her life. If I don't report her missing, *no one* will.

She doesn't have family here—at least none I've ever heard about. She's always been so clingy, and maybe now I understand why. I might be her *only* friend outside of work. Paul, our boss, lives in his mom's basement and I doubt he'd take anything seriously unless it walked in and smacked him upside the head.

I want to scream. I want to run out of here and find them myself. I hate sitting on this scratchy, dust-scented couch, wasting time.

Mom has told me about a hundred times today that she's not letting me out of her sight until this thing is over. If she hadn't come to town, I'd already be out there searching. Or maybe I'd be in jail for supposedly murdering the people I care about. Either way—I wouldn't be *here*.

Mom walks over and drops a hotel key into my hand.

"I got everything situated. He tried to tell me they were fully booked tonight for any rooms with more than one bed. *Does he think I'm stupid?* This is *not* a five-star resort. No one stays here if they have other options."

She looks *so* proud of herself, and it makes me laugh—just a little.

"Alright," she says, grabbing her purse. "Let's go get situated and then pick that brain of yours for the information we need."

She's far too confident in me.

SEVENTEEN

The hotel mattress utterly sucks compared to my overly used, formed-to-fit-my-body, perfectly comfortable bed back at home. My room isn't big enough to fit a cute reading chair, so I always just sit or lie in my bed. Most of my days off are spent bed-rotting with my latest book.

Mom's in the bathroom, changing into something more comfortable. We just bought my clothes at the store, so they don't even smell fresh, but I'm just happy to be out of the outfit I was wearing the night Matt disappeared. It feels like that night was weeks ago—even though it just happened.

Our hotel room is small, which we expected based on the size of the building. We each have a "queen"-sized mattress with a tiny nightstand between them. There's a lamp with a pull chain and a crusty beige phone that connects to the front desk—home of Mom's favorite tattooed clerk. The artwork above the beds looks like it was painted by a three-year-old, but there's something weirdly charming about it.

Each bed has a slightly discolored orange comforter and scratchy tan sheets. Mom already did a full inspection for bed bugs and didn't find anything, but I guarantee we'll both be itching for weeks anyway. The TV on the wall only has four channels: weather, old westerns, music, and the news. Which we *will not* be watching, because I'm sure my face will show up sooner or later.

Our town is small, and hotel options are limited. If she'd known I wouldn't be allowed back home, she would never have booked this place. She only intended to stay here for the night, just long enough to assess the situation before coming to stay with me.

"Your father would die if he saw this place, wouldn't he?" she says with a grimace, then winces. "Sorry. That was insensitive."

"No, it's okay. He'd definitely have a thing or two to say about it," I mutter, glancing around with a disgusted look.

Mom does the same and shakes her head. "I guess it'll do for tonight. Tomorrow, I'll make other arrangements, okay?"

She walks over and sits on her bed, which lets out the most god-awful squealing sound I've ever heard. We both gasp and jump.

"Oh my *God*," she wheezes, and we both burst into uncontrollable laughter. Belly laughing, tears forming in our eyes.

"This is going to be some story to tell your father."

"He's going to be *so* sad he missed out on the luxury we're living in right now," I giggle, wiping a tear from the corner of my eye.

The laughter fades, and I watch her expression turn serious again.

"Okay, honey. We need to walk through everything again. I know you told the cops and Claire as much as you could remember, but I really think if we sit here in this dim lighting, surrounded by these tin-foil comforters, you might recall something else. Something small but important. Something that might point the investigation away from you."

She's right about the comforter. It crinkles every time I move like I'm wrapped in foil.

I nod, even though I don't want to do this. But she has a point. I'm not always great at remembering little details—and sometimes, little details are what solve crimes.

"I'm just going to sit here with you in silence for a few minutes," she says softly, "so you can breathe and relax your body. Let me know when you're ready, and I'll guide you if you need me to, okay?"

She shifts to sit cross-legged on the bed. I close my eyes and take a breath. When everything happened with the twins' family, we all went to therapy together. The shrink taught my parents that I might need these kinds of grounding exercises. Back then, they didn't help much. I was too shut down. But now… maybe they'll work. I'm not a kid anymore. Maybe I'm not *as* afraid of my own thoughts.

Starting at the top of my head, I begin relaxing each part of my body on the way down.

Face.

Breathe.

Neck.

Breathe.

Shoulders.

Breathe.

Arms and hands.

Breathe.

Chest.

Breathe.

Back.

Breathe.

Hips.

Breathe.

Legs and feet.

Breathe.

I hear Mom breathing with me. Focusing on the physical is so much easier than diving into the mental chaos.

I give her a small nod—now or never.

"I'm going to help you go back. Are you ready?" she asks gently. Even in that soft tone, her voice makes me flinch. I nod again.

"You're lying in your bed. It's raining really hard outside. The power's out, so there's no fan, no AC—no background noise. Just the storm. You pick up your phone and start scrolling. Do you hear anything?"

"No. Nothing."

"Slow down. Don't answer so fast. Try again. Go back. *Listen* to the house. You know what belongs—and what doesn't."

I lie in silence, focusing. If I'd heard something, I *would* have jumped out of bed and investigated. Right?

I take a deep breath.

"Nothing... Wait. There *was* a click. A small click." My voice is slow, hesitant. "I was listening to the rain. Thinking about Bridgette and her family. How we used to play in the rain and make mud castles."

My eyes fly open. I sit up and lock eyes with my mom. I see her start to tear up at the mention of Bridgette.

"Mom, I think I heard the front door open. That means someone *was* in the house. Someone *did* walk in!"

"Alice," she says calmly, "lay down and breathe. Don't react yet. Stay with me. You need to stay in that place mentally. We're not done."

I nod, swallowing hard, and lay back down.

I *heard* the door open. Moments before Matt arrived at the house—someone else was already inside.

Now I just have to prove it.

EIGHTEEN

Mom is asking questions about how I feel in different scenarios she's creating—things like what I see or hear while working a normal shift or reading a book at home. Just trying to keep my mind focused.

Every so often, she slips in something about what happened the other night.

Her concern about Matt seems to have grown since I told her more about the creepy stalker situation. I was a little nervous she'd be upset with me for not telling her sooner how it had gotten worse, but she was surprisingly understanding.

Probably because, in her mind, it's not *super* creepy—just creepy enough to make me look over my shoulder getting into my car.

"After the smiley face appeared on the sauce jar, you drove to Matt's work, right? The bookstore?" she asks.

"Yes. I drove to the bookstore because I needed someone level-headed to tell me I wasn't being irrational—and that someone was actually messing with me."

"And when you got there, was he as comforting as you expected? Did he calm you?"

I sigh. This one isn't just a yes or no answer. "Normally he would have been, but this time he wasn't... because it was the anniversary of his mom's disappearance."

She pauses. I don't think I've told her much about what happened to Matt's mom. If she asks, I'll definitely be telling her it's not something I want to talk about.

"When you walked into the bookstore, what did you see? Smell? Hear?"

Thank *God* she caught on to my reluctance.

"It's one of my favorite places to walk into. The smell of books smacks you in the face the second the door opens and the bell dings. When I walked in, I saw

Matt come out from behind the counter, asking why I was there since I was supposed to be at work."

"Did you tell him what happened?"

"Yes."

"How did he respond?"

"He seemed... irritated that I was making a big deal about the sauce. Said a coworker probably did it, or someone from a nearby aisle was eavesdropping and wanted to pull a prank."

"How did that make you feel?"

"Honestly? Stupid. Embarrassed. It shut me down pretty fast. I told him he was probably right and didn't argue—I just wanted to go home."

"Did you leave after that?"

"I *started* to. But then the coffee cup on my car stopped me."

"Wait... what coffee cup?" Mom sounds completely confused now.

I sit up and explain how I walked out to a coffee cup sitting on top of my car. I tell her how I didn't remember stopping, but Matt said I must've been so dissociated that my muscle memory took over and I stopped for coffee without realizing it. Her face flushes with shock.

"He said *that*?" she asks, her voice tight.

Now *I'm* confused. "Yeah? And he was probably right. I could've just zoned out, stopped, and not remembered it."

"You really believe you went into a coffee shop, ordered a drink, stood in line waiting for it, and then drove the rest of the way to the bookstore with absolutely *no* recollection of it?!"

Her tone is pure disbelief.

"Well… I *did*, for about an hour or so. Until I got home." I suddenly feel dumb just saying it.

"What happened when you got home, Alice?"

She's flipped from comforting to protective *real* fast.

"I emptied the coffee into the sink, went about my business, and then… later, when I passed the trash, I noticed the cardboard sleeve had slid down when I tossed it. You know, the thing they put on to keep your hand from getting burned?"

"…Yes?"

"Well, under it… there was a smiley face drawn on the cup."

Her hand jolts up to her mouth and she lets out a sharp gasp.

"Alice, *please* tell me you told the cop about this!"

"I did. His team was still at my house when he called them, and they found the cup in the trash. It was bagged as evidence."

She takes a deep breath and looks relieved—but then her eyes shift as if her thoughts are loading again. I wait for her next question.

"You said something that makes me want to ask a question… but I don't want you to get upset when I ask it, okay?"

Uh-oh. I don't like that one bit.

"Okay, ask away," I say, hesitantly.

"Was your back turned to your car when Matt went to the back of the bookstore? For that customer?"

I just stare at her.

What is she implying?

"Yes. I was reading that new children's book while waiting for him."

"How long was he in the back? Long enough to put a coffee on top of your car?"

"Mom, you *can't* be serious."

"It's just a question, that's all. I know Matthew means a lot to you, but that might mean you don't *see* his flaws. I'm your mother, and I'm not going to rule out a single person right now."

I cannot *believe* her.

He's the only one who's been there for me these past few months. He's kind, gentle, understanding—and he was *attacked* and *taken*. How can she even *imply* that he might be behind any of this?

"The main reason my mind went there," she continues, "is because your lawyer told me that all the muddy shoe prints in your house belonged to Matt's boots. He walked all over your house before coming upstairs to tell you—barefoot—that someone had broken in. There's no sign of forced entry, and he had a key. It's… odd."

We sit in silence.

She just watches me while I stare at the wall, trying to process what she's said. My mother is basically suggesting that *Matt* is the one who's been messing with me.

That maybe he's framing me for his own murder.

Even though she makes some unsettling points, she's still wrong.

I don't know how Matt's shoes made those muddy tracks. I don't know how someone else got into my house without leaving evidence behind.

I don't know why only my fingerprints are *everywhere*.

I don't know a lot of things.

But I *do* know Matt.

And he didn't do this.

He couldn't have.

NINETEEN

Today we're going back to the police station to speak with the detective in charge of this whole case. They still believe I'm a suspect, but we're going to try and prove that I've done nothing wrong.

We also need to inform them about Chris's whereabouts—or lack thereof, actually.

I still haven't heard from her, and on the way into the station we stopped at her house again. There was still no sign that she'd been there. I wish I'd spat on that stupid smiley face when I had the chance.

I think again about how she has *literally* no one. She once told me she was an only child, and both her parents had no siblings either.

So, when they passed away, she was completely alone. She moved here to get away from the city that reminded her of all she'd lost, and she found herself falling in love with small-town life. She always said it was like having a family—the way she could remember most of the customers' names, how the same people would come in day after day.

I guess she was right in a way. The small-town vibe does make for a kind of intimate lifestyle, especially compared to life in the city.

I used to hate how everyone here knew my name and face, but right now I'm realizing I actually don't mind it at all.

I can't imagine how this place affected Matt when his mom went missing. To know that every single person you come into contact with *knows* exactly what's happening in your life… it sounds like a nightmare.

I bet they all gave him those same sympathetic puppy-dog eyes and a pat on the back. I wonder if he appreciated it—or if he hated it as much as I think he did.

God, I hope he's okay.

As we pull into the station, I notice there are too many cars out front, and it pisses me off. Why aren't more of them out *looking* for him?!

They better get their asses in gear the second I tell them about Chris, or I might lose it and end up in a psych ward today.

I hear my phone buzz.

A text from Paul.

"Still nothing from Christina. I hope you've heard from her. Let me know if there's anything I can do to help."

"I haven't heard from her either. Just got to the station to speak with the detective and will let them know she's possibly missing as well. If you see a random number calling you today, please answer. It might be him verifying she hasn't been to work. Thanks."

"Got it. Ringer turned up. Let me know what he says."

I shove my phone into the glove box. Mom gives me a look of confusion.

"I don't know if they've found more planted evidence that could get me arrested today, but I'm not taking any chances. Keep my phone close to you, just in case Chris calls. Please."

She nods in understanding, and we head into the station.

The front room is so outdated it's honestly gross. There's wood paneling on the walls *and* ceiling, wrapping all the way around the front desk. The tile floor probably used to be a nice marble, but now it's beige and brown from years of foot traffic. They could at least dust and mop the place once in a while.

Detective Harper is leaning against the counter, chatting with the front desk clerk. His head turns when we walk in, and that same sly smile creeps me out to my core.

"Well hello, Alice," he says. "Didn't expect you back so soon. Where's your lawyer friend?"

"She'll be here soon," Mom answers before I can. "We need to report something now, so we didn't want to wait."

"Oh? Alright then. Come with me—we'll get you situated in a room so we can chat." He nods to the clerk, who buzzes us in.

He leads us into a room with a table and five mismatched black office chairs. The walls are a hideous pale yellow that looks like it was used in every public building in town.

There's a black-and-white abstract painting on the far wall that clashes completely with the color scheme. The carpet is just as grimy and brownish as the lobby tiles. Maybe this is where they hold case briefings or staff meetings.

"Would either of you like something to drink? Water? Coffee? I can make a fresh pot."

I don't buy his nice act.

"A water for both of us would be lovely, thank you," Mom says without even looking at him.

He walks out and leaves us alone in silence.

We don't speak.

The quiet is suffocating.

The only sound is the tick of a cheap wall clock.

tick tock … tick tock …

I hyperfocus on the sound, and when he comes back a few minutes later, I practically jump out of my skin as the door creaks open. He hands us each a water bottle, sets a pen and notepad in front of himself, and does the same for me.

He settles into his chair with a big breath.

"Alright," he says. "What are we reporting today?"

tick tock … tick tock …

Mom looks to me, like she's giving me permission to speak. I hate that, but I'll ignore it for now. I pull the pen and notepad closer, inhale deeply, and steady my thoughts.

"My coworker and best friend, Christina, is missing as well."

I feel my voice crack. The lump in my throat swells. The second I say *best friend,* I feel my mom's head snap toward me in surprise. I haven't called anyone that since the twins.

"Uh, okay," the detective says. "How long has it been since you've seen or spoken with her?"

"No one has seen or heard from her since the day you picked me up at the hospital. I saw her in the parking lot, on the phone with my mom, while I was in your car. Apparently, that was the last time anyone heard from her."

"So once again… another person goes missing, and *you* are the last person to see or speak with them."

tick tock … tick tock …

Shit.

I should've known he'd go there. My concern for Chris totally overrode my common sense. I should've waited for my lawyer.

"Yes," I say. "But just listen to me. We work together at the market. My boss called yesterday and asked if I'd heard from her. We drove by her house— nothing. No one was there. Do you remember what I told you about the smiley face?"

"Yes. I remember." He's not buying it, but I don't care.

"There was one drawn out front. On the sidewalk. In yellow chalk. Whoever's doing this took Matt, and I *genuinely* believe they took Chris too. We came today because I'm afraid. I think I might be next."

Tears fall. My mom rubs my back while the detective scribbles notes.

"Alright. I'm going to humor this," he finally says. "Only because this case is eating up my entire schedule. What's her address?"

tick… tock… tick… tock…

***

After what feels like an eternity, the detective returns. Claire's finally here, but somehow that doesn't make me feel any safer.

"I spoke with your boss," he begins. "His story matches yours—no one's seen or heard from Christina since the hospital. We've put a BOLO out on her car and checked the address you gave me. My team sent me pictures of the sidewalk."

He looks straight at me.

"There's no chalk smiley face."

"It *was* there. I saw it too," my mom chimes in, looking to me. "Is this the kind of bizarre stuff that's been happening to you? Things just… disappearing?"

I nod.

If only she knew.

The little things that make me feel like I'm losing my mind—almost daily. The subtle shifts. The objects moved. The unease.

She meets my eyes. Her expression softens.

"Oh, honey. I'm sorry for not believing you."

Tears threaten again, but I push them back. We don't have time for this.

"It *was* there," I repeat. "My mom saw it. Just one more reason for you to believe I didn't do any of this. You're wasting time. We need to find Matt and Chris!"

The detective nods slowly. "Listen. I'm not saying you're off the hook. Because you're not. But I'm not arresting you—not yet. We'll continue investigating the mayor's son's disappearance and now your friend's as well. Don't leave town. You're still a suspect. I'll call you when we know more."

I nod again, grateful to at least be walking out of here—for now.

"Go back to your hotel," he says. "Just wait for my call."

He turns to Claire. "Apologies that you made the trip for nothing. Once I have more, we'll continue with questioning."

She shakes his hand. "I understand. I know this is a small town, and you may do things differently here, but I do appreciate you taking her seriously."

He shrugs. "If this wasn't the mayor's son, we wouldn't be handling it this way. He's not going to be happy that she's still walking free. She's lucky I believe her."

He leaves the room.

We pack up and follow, heading back to the hotel.

My chest feels tight again.

Please, let them find Chris.

TWENTY

It's been two days. I can't believe I've been stuck in this hotel room for *two whole days*. Just sitting around. Waiting. For something. Anything. I can't stand this. I should be out there *looking* for them myself.

They've apparently called in more teams from other counties to help with the search for Mayor Ward's son. Suddenly, the man actually cares about the well-being of his child.

The detective told me they're searching for Chris too—but I feel like no one even cares about her. They're all just focused on Matt so they can be the one to find him and get the credit. I'm sure his dad promised a big promotion or raise to whoever brings him back. It's all about *climbing the ladder* here.

This town is such a joke. Matt's dad hasn't shown *this* much interest in him since the day I met Matt. From what I know, he hasn't given a shit since Matt's mom disappeared when he was a kid. There was always someone else around to raise him, so his father didn't have to.

He became mayor just to say he'd "make sure nothing like this ever happens again in our town." But he hasn't actually done anything to stop it. He dove headfirst into his career and pretended his son didn't exist.

Matt has told me so many stories about how, once he turned 18, he went out of his way to investigate what happened to his mom. He even hired a private investigator. But the trail always ran cold. The only thing they ever found was her abandoned car at the train station in the next town over.

The car was spotless. Completely empty. They searched for her for *months*. In the end, they claimed she just packed up and left because she couldn't handle being a mother anymore.

Matt told me that was bullshit. He and his mom were best friends. They did everything together. She would've never just left him like that. He's convinced his father had something to do with it—maybe blackmailed her or scared her off somehow.

He still swears he'll find her one day. And honestly? I believe him.

I'm lying on this rock-hard mattress watching the weather channel when I hear my mom's phone ring. She'd just gone out for some fresh air. Said she needed to stretch her legs, clear her head. She laced up her running shoes, so I figured she'd be gone about twenty minutes.

It's only been ten, but… she left her phone. That makes me uneasy.

I glance at the screen. It's the detective. I answer it on speaker.

"H–Hello? Did you find them?!" The words tumble out before I can even think.

"Alice?" the detective replies. "I tried your phone first, but you didn't answer."

"Oh—sorry, I didn't hear it ring. I was just…
zoning out. Trying not to think too hard." I start pacing
between the beds.

"We found her car." His tone is calm, too calm.

My chest tightens. I can't breathe.

"Y–You found *whose* car?" I already know the
answer. But I ask anyway.

"Christina's. We found it about an hour ago.
There's no sign of her yet—which is good. That means
we have a lead. And it means you were telling the truth."

I stop in my tracks, frozen.

"I don't have any more details just yet," he
continues, "but I wanted you to know… I believe you.
You're not crazy, Alice. She's out there somewhere.
And I *will* find both her and Matthew."

He sounds… sincere. Like a totally different man.
Not like the one who *accused* me. The one who was so
sure I was guilty.

He has every reason to arrest me. My fingerprints
are on the supposed weapon. There's blood in my
house. No sign of forced entry.

At this point... I'm starting to wonder if I *did* do this.

"Alice? Did you hear me?" he asks.

"Yes. I'm sorry. I heard you." My breath is shallow and tight.

Suddenly, the hotel door creaks open. I about jump out of my skin, startled so badly that I gasp—and inhale my own spit. Now I'm coughing uncontrollably, gasping, trying to breathe.

"Alice! What happened?! Are you okay?" My mom's voice cuts through the chaos as I double over, holding up the phone for her to take.

"Hello? Is someone there?!" the detective shouts, panicked. Probably thinking the person he's after has found me.

"I'm her mother," Mom says, panting a little from her jog. "She's okay. Just choked. Hold on."

I'm still hunched over, gasping. Tears stream down my cheeks—not from crying, but from pure lack of oxygen.

"Thank God," the detective exhales. "I thought... never mind. I was just calling to inform your daughter we found her friend's car. No sign of her yet. Since she has no family, I promised Alice I'd keep her informed. If I get any other updates I can share, you'll be the first to know."

"Thank you, Detective. Have a good day." She hangs up and turns to me, hands on her hips.

"What in the world just happened?! I came back for my phone and find you choking to death on air! Do you need water?"

My voice is hoarse as I wipe my face. "I'm sorry. I guess I'm more on edge than I thought. You scared the hell out of me coming in like that."

We lock eyes—and then burst out laughing. Like, *full-on* laughing.

"Jesus. I don't know what to do with you sometimes," Mom giggles.

"Well, maybe next time you leave the room, *don't* leave your phone behind and my thoughts won't go straight to worst-case scenario!"

"No, you're right. I didn't mean to leave it. I'll be more cautious. The last thing I need is for something to happen and you not be able to reach me."

Just like that, the laughter fades. Reality rushes back in.

"Mom…" I say, quieter now. "Do you think this person could be after me too?"

She sits down beside me, the bed crunching beneath her weight.

"I don't know, honey. All we can do is wait. And pray. Pray they find them… and figure out who's trying to frame you."

We sit in silence. For once, it's not awkward. Just… still.

Then my phone buzzes on the nightstand.

"Huh. That's odd," I say.

"What is it?" Mom asks.

"It's a text. From the detective, already."

I pick it up. Open it. And feel the blood drain from my face.

"Got a little more information. They found her car abandoned. At the train station. Next town over. Looks like she skipped town. Will text if I know more."

My voice is barely a whisper. "Oh God. They're never going to find her."

"Don't say that! They *will* find her!" Mom's voice is fierce, but I shake my head.

"No, Mom. You don't understand. This is *exactly* what happened to Matt's mom. When he was a kid. And she was never found. Still, to this day—nothing. She just *vanished*."

I watch as the color drains from her face, just like it did mine. I set my phone down and let out a slow, shallow breath.

We both sit in silence, staring at nothing.

Waiting.

Hoping.

Dreading.

TWENTY ONE

I can't sleep. I've been lying here counting the weird grooves on the ceiling for hours. I roll on my side, take a slow breath, and close my eyes.

When I was a kid, I always dreamt of growing up and becoming someone important. Someone that others would lean on and look up to for guidance or advice. I pictured being a teacher, or a counselor, maybe even working for the government.

Never in my wildest dreams did I think I would live in a small town working for minimum wage at a local grocery store. I also never thought I would fall in love and then have that man ripped from me by some lunatic. Or that I would become best friends with the funniest, kindest person on the planet and then lose her to some black hole somewhere.

I spent so many months wishing that Chris would just leave me alone and stop yapping in my ear every lunch break. Now all I want is to hear some wild and juicy story about whatever show she's obsessed with, or some hot dude she saw at the coffee shop. I would do anything to hear her voice right now.

I put on such a front that she did nothing but got on my nerves but in all honesty, she was the truest friend I've ever had. I've told her barely anything about myself but the little she does know, she remembers and holds close.

Every holiday she would make me some sort of gift.

Every hard day at work, I would come back from break to my favorite coffee.

She listened, she didn't judge, and she saw me for who I was. My favorite thing about her was how she would try to force me to be social with her. Go to the movies, out to dinners, literally anything.

She knew if she didn't *try* I would just stay cooped up in my house with my books and my bed forever.

I never thanked her enough for that.

When I lost the twins I closed my heart down with barbed wire and picket fencing. There was never going to be a day that I would ever let myself feel that kind of pain again.

Way back then I couldn't sleep one night and went downstairs for a glass of water. I overheard my parents talking, this was the night after the funeral, and my dad was a blubbering mess saying how it was his fault.

How he should have caught onto the signs and stepped in sooner. How if he would have just reported everything to the cops they would still be here.

After that he and I grew apart pretty quickly. I leaned more on my mom when I had to, if I had to. Other than that I just stuck to myself and kept my head down.

I don't know what signs he saw or what information he had that could have stopped that man from hurting them, but I was angry for a very long time that he didn't do anything about it like he said.

Two weeks after I graduated high school my parents told me they were moving out of town and starting fresh in a bigger city. They asked if I wanted to come with them and start fresh too but I said no. This was my home and I was not meant for big city living.

The thought of having to start over and meeting new people made my skin crawl. Everyone here already knew my story and avoided me at all costs, why would I want that to change?!

I was perfectly satisfied with how everyone already looked at me as the girl who's got trauma deeper than the Grand Canyon. It made my desire to be ignored and left alone an easy task to manage.

I spoke to my manager at the store and told him my situation and ended up getting a raise and more hours. I was able to afford to rent my small house, even if that meant not getting to eat 3 full meals some days.

I told myself everyone starts somewhere and this is just the starting line for me.

My parents moved and my mom told me we had to maintain weekly coffee dates, which we have via facetime. I rarely spoke to my dad after they left which I honestly didn't mind.

I still don't.

Maybe one day I'll muster up enough courage to ask the question I have been holding onto for so long, but not yet.

***

After the detective called and we sat in silence, my mom turned and looked at me and asked if after all of this I would be willing to move to the city with them now. I told her I don't think I can. When they find Matt and Chris they're going to need me here and I'm not willing to abandon them.

She didn't like that answer but it was the best one I had. I knew what she was thinking, what if they never find them? What happens when they do and it's not a good outcome? Will I still stay then?

She didn't ask that, but I could see she wanted to. But to answer those questions, I don't know. I really just don't know.

There's no way they don't ever find them. I know when Matts mom disappeared there wasn't as much technology in the crime field as there is now. I believe they'll find something, anything, like a fiber of clothing, or even a small hair. Then everything will work out.

I think back to all the articles I read online when I found out about Matt's mom. How there was no reason to believe that she would up and walk away, but there was no evidence or leads to suggest otherwise. Her car was wiped clean and empty, just like Chris's. She didn't leave behind a note or anything for someone to find. She didn't ever tell a single soul she didn't want to be with her son. But yet, they assume she just walked away.

That just doesn't sit right with me. I know they looked and followed small tips for about a year and then Matt took it into his own hands but it just doesn't seem right. If that was my own mother, my father would have never ever given up. He would be spending the rest of his life searching for her. So why has Matt's dad just moved on with his life? It's not right.

Chris's car being found in the same way as Matt's moms, has my head in a whirlwind. I have so many questions that need answered I can't think straight. Like what do they mean wiped clean? Are even her own fingerprints gone because that makes me believe someone else would have cleaned it. Not her. She wouldn't take the time to drive to a train station and *clean her car* of any evidence of herself and then just leave?

Then again, why would Matt's mom do that too? Something's just not right. Either someone kidnapped his mom and that same person is back and took Chris or … there is no 'or'… there's no other option. Someone took them and if the cops don't hurry up and find her, the case is going to go cold and this person could go back into hiding for another 20ish years!

Someone *has* to do something more. I have to do something more. I sit up and reach for my shoes. I'm going to go find her. She deserves me out there looking for her. So does Matt and I already know I won't sleep until they are found.

As I'm tying my laces my mom starts to wake up. *Shit.*

"Alice?" She says sleepily. "What are you doing?" She sits up while rubbing her eyes and sees my shoe in my hand. I was so close.

"Mom, go back to sleep."

"Whoa, what are you doing?! You think you can just leave in the middle of the night without me? What the hell Alice!"

Welp, she's fully awake and alert now.

"I have to help! I have to be out there doing something. I can't just lie here waiting for someone to call me or someone to come kidnap me! I'm going insane!" I didn't mean to be so loud but I'm practically shouting.

"Take that damn shoe off before I rip it off your foot. People are missing! MISSING." We are both on our feet now. "Something has happened and the cops are doing everything they can! You going out there will do NOTHING TO HELP! I am NOT going to lose you too!" Guess we both don't care if we wake the neighbors at this point.

"Oh yeah?! YOU CARE?! Sitting around doesn't do anything mom! WE. HAVE. TO. HELP! We can't just sit here and turn our cheeks like you and dad did with the twins!"

Instant regret. We both gasp at my words. I throw my hand up to my mouth and wish I could take it back.

147

Her face is pale. My mouth is so dry I can't swallow. We just stand still in shock for what feels like an eternity.

Quietly, with what sounds like defeat in her voice, she says, "I understand you're frustrated. I know you want to fix it. But… We have to stay here. You have to stay safe. I have to keep you safe." Tears swell up and pour over onto her face.

"I'm sorry mom. I shouldn't have said that." I'm starring at a spot on the floor, not blinking, barely breathing. My head is spinning so fast I fell like I might pass out.

"Don't be sorry. You're not wrong. We could have done more back then. That is probably a conversation we should have already had but now is not the time. It's 3 in the morning. We need to sleep so we can have half a brain tomorrow."

She's wiping her tears and sitting back down on her bed. I sit down too and take my one shoe that I managed to get on, back off. I swallow the lump in my throat and try to blink the sting away in my eyes.

I can't believe I let myself say that to her. She didn't deserve it no matter how true it was.

My phone lights up. It's the detective. Mom and I lock eyes and she can see the panic on my face as I answer it and put it on speaker.

"Hello?" I say with a shaking voice. I'm assuming the worst.

Why else would he call me in the middle of the night.

"Hey Alice, sorry if I woke you. This just couldn't wait until morning. They think they found Matthew. We called his father but no answer. I think you should get up there so he's not alone."

He's alive.

TWENTY TWO

The hospital hallway feels colder than I expected, the fluorescent lights flickering overhead as I hurry through the maze of white walls and linoleum floors. My heart's pounding so loudly I'm sure the nurses can hear it from down the hall.

Matt.

He's alive.

The words echo over and over in my mind, but even as relief washes over me, a knot of fear tightens in my stomach. What if he not the same Matt who disappeared that night? What if the person who took him wasn't finished and I'm still next? There are so many unanswered questions, it's making it difficult to even feel a sense of relief that he's here.

I push open the door to the ICU and there he is.. lying still, pale, hooked up to tubes and machines that are thankfully beeping steadily. His hair is damp against his forehead, and his chest rises slowly with each breath.

I glance around, looking for his father, but he's nowhere to be seen. How could he not be here already? He was called before me. Of course, he's taking his time. I wouldn't expect anything less of that man.

I rush to his side and grab his hand. He flinches his hands back and his eyes flutter open, and he looks right at me. He smiles slightly in relief when our eyes meet and I feel my shoulders drop. He's trying to say something but I can't understand, his lips are barely moving. I lean in closer, taking his hand in mine. It was warm, but weak. So weak.

"Matt," I whisper through tears. "It's me. Alice."

He blinks a few times, then mutters, "She… kept talking.. about my Mom…"

I feel my eyebrows scrunch in confusion and a chill down my spine. I kiss his hand in mine and something catches my eye on his wrist. There, small but clear, was a smiley face burned into his skin.

My breath caught in my throat. This wasn't over. I gently squeezed his hand and try to focus. "Who's *she*, Matt? Who kept talking about your mom?"

His eyes flutter shut again. His breathing was shallow, uneven. A nurse rushes in, checking the monitors and adjusting the IV. The once steady beeping begins to falter.

"Is he going to be okay?" I asked, my voice trembling.

The nurse smiled kindly but with a practiced calm. "He's stable for now. Like I told the police, and his father, he just needs some rest."

I nodded, but my mind was racing.

Who was 'she'?

The tiny smiley face on his wrist is stuck in my thoughts. I pull my phone out and snap a quick picture, just in case.

The detective's words replayed again: *They think they found Matthew.* Found... but by who? And why had they left that mark?

Everything in me wants to scream, to ask him a hundred questions. But all I can do is sit by his bedside, hold his hand, and hope Matt will wake up soon enough to tell me the truth. Whatever happened, it wasn't just about Matt, or me, but also somehow his mother? I'm starting to realize this is much bigger than I thought it was.

I wait a few moments before speaking again, softer this time. "Matt… do you remember what you were trying to say? About your mom?"

His brow furrowed, and he blinks slowly, as if trying to pull something from deep inside his mind.

"I… don't know," he whispers, voice barely audible. "It's all… fuzzy. I can't remember. I'm sorry."

Panic bubbles up inside me, twisting my chest. "It's okay, Matt. Just take your time. I'm not going anywhere."

He squeezes my hand weakly, but his eyes are distant, clouded. "I want to remember. I want to tell you… but it's like there's a wall."

The nurse reappears and gently reminds me that he needs rest and quiet. I nod, reluctant to leave, but know I can't push him too hard. As she dims the lights, I stay seated beside him, my mind racing faster than ever.

If Matt can't remember, then the answers have to be somewhere else. Somewhere I haven't looked yet. Now I know, somehow, this all links back to his mother's disappearance. And the smiley face on his wrist? Whatever it meant, it was a clue, meant for me, and one I wasn't going to ignore. Not this time.

***

The next morning, running on hospital caffeine, I convince my mother to let me free from her chains for a few hours. I told her I was going to be at the hospital all day with Matt and there wasn't anyway someone was going to kidnap me there. The place is full of cameras, so she agreed to let me take the car as long as I called her when I arrived.

I stop by and check on him and call her so she can hear the beeping of the machines. I kiss his forehead and make my way to The Escape Room. When I pull in I see a young girl behind the counter, they must have had someone come in to cover his shifts so they wouldn't lose the store.

Walking in, she smiles at me, "Alice! I remember you! Matt's girlfriend right? I heard he's safe and in the hospital! How are you holding up?"

I can't remember this girl's name to save my life, but I smile and nod my head.

"Yeah, he's good. I'm good too, thanks for asking! But, hey…" I lower my voice due to someone browsing in one of the isles. "I need a small favor. Matt's really down and I thought maybe if I brought him something of his from here it might help cheer him up a bit. Would you mind letting me in the back office for a second? I'll be quick I promise."

She smiles and nods and hands me the key.

Bingo, I'm in.

I open the door to his small, cluttered, office that's still *mostly* untouched since he vanished. The familiar scent of old paper and cheap coffee still lingers in the air.

I hesitate for a moment before stepping inside. This feels wrong, like I'm invading his privacy, but I need answers. If Matt's memories were locked away behind a fog, maybe his belongings could tell me what his mind couldn't and point me in the right direction. Someone has to find Christina.

I search through his desk drawers and find a handful of crumpled receipts, a worn notebook, and a faded map tucked beneath a stack of invoices. The notebook caught my eye first. Its dark leather cover was cracked and soft, and inside, there were pages filled with scribbled notes, dates, and names — most of which I didn't understand. I shove it all into my bag and run out to my car, thanking the girl at the front counter as I run out.

I drive to a random parking lot and grab my bag and hope I find some sort of connection in Matt's notebook. I turn through page after page and most of it makes absolutely no sense. It seems its mainly work related but a few pages here and there are him writing down thoughts.

Then I see it: an address underlined twice, with a small smiley face doodled beside it. I notice the date on the page is the same day he got super defensive with me about the coffee on my car. His mood on that day makes sense now. I start to wonder if the same person who's been taunting me, has also been taunting him. Why wouldn't he tell me?

The address was unfamiliar, except that it was somewhere in the next town over. The same town that they found Chris's car, and his mother's car.

My heart skips a beat.

Could this be where Christina is? Was Matt lured to this location that day?

I grab the map and trace my finger along the roads to the neighboring town, my mind already racing with possibilities. I have to get there. I have to find out what Matt was trying to say before the memory slipped away forever. I shove the notebook and map back into my bag and head out.

***

The drive was a blur. My thoughts raced faster than the road under my tires. Questions piled up in my mind, but there was one thing I knew for sure, whatever I found here could change everything.

The address led me to an older office building. I parked a few doors down and stepped out, the late afternoon sun casting long shadows across the pavement.

As I approach the front doors, my heart begins pounding in my chest. The air feels heavy, like it's also holding its breath, waiting.

Then, just as I reach the steps, I see it, etched faintly in the concrete, a single chalk smiley face staring back at me.

A shiver ran down my spine.

This was no coincidence.

This was a message meant for me.

TWENTY THREE

The police didn't call. They showed up.

Mr. Detective Man is standing on my front porch with another officer I don't recognize, both of them grim-faced and quiet. My mother standing behind me like a silent shield.

"We need to speak with you, Alice. About Matthew."

My stomach dropped.

Inside, the detective is pacing like he's stalling, buying time for me to crumble before he'll even get the words out. He finally stops and glances toward his partner, then back to me.

"We've started digging deeper into Matthew Ward's history. There were some sealed juvenile records. His father had them expunged, or at least buried. But in light of recent events… they've been reopened."

"What kind of history?" I asked, heart pounding in my throat.

The younger officer clears his throat and opens a manila file. "A few years ago, before you and Matt started dating, he was charged with breaking and entering, harassment, and trespassing. All involving a girl he had been seeing at the time. Her name's been redacted for now."

"No, that's—no." I shake my head, standing. "That doesn't sound like him."

Harper doesn't flinch. "The report describes an escalating pattern, Alice. He'd show up at her work, her house, leave notes. She ended up filing a restraining order. His father intervened before it went to court."

"He was a kid," I whisper.

"He was seventeen," he corrects. "Old enough to know better."

My mother crosses her arms tightly over her chest. "That's it. You're done. You're not going back to that hospital. Not around him. Not until we know more."

I turn to her, my voice low. "Mom, you don't know him. This doesn't sound right—"

160

"This is exactly what sounds right, Alice," she snapped, voice shaking with rage. "You've been defending a boy who vanished without a trace, and now magically reappears with trauma and no memory? Covered in bruises and creepy drawings branded into his skin?" She points down at my phone still clutched in my hand. "He's dangerous. You just don't want to see it."

"DID YOU GO THROUGH MY PHONE?!" I scream at her. She throws her hands up like I didn't hear a word she just said.

I swallow hard, but the detective's voice keeps replaying in my head…

Harassment.

Restraining order.

Breaking and entering.

All things that hit too close to what's currently happening now.

Was that what he was trying to tell me at the hospital? Was he trying to confess?

"Maybe," my mom adds softly, eyes now pleading, "maybe all of this… the break-ins, the disappearances, even Christina… maybe it *is* him. Maybe losing his

161

mother the way he did broke something inside of him, Alice. You of all people understand that."

I know she didn't just compare Matt to the *twins father*. I don't have a response. I can't possibly form one. I don't believe a word she's saying, but I also don't know if she's wrong.

I can't breathe.

My mother's words echoed like static in my skull.

He's dangerous…

Maybe it's all him…

But it's not just her voice anymore. It's the detective. It's Matt's silence. It's the damn smiley face. I'm getting dizzy and the walls start to feel like they're closing in.

I want to scream. I want to scream at my mother for judging someone she doesn't even know. I want to scream at the detective for digging up dirt and calling it the truth. I want to scream at Matt for keeping secrets.

But mostly, I want to scream at myself. For believing again. For letting someone in, when I swore I never would. Because this is what happens.

People disappear. People lie. People hurt you and leave you behind with your heart in your hands.

Maybe I should've listened to the warning signs. Maybe this is my fault too. Before I know what I'm doing, I grab my bag and keys off the table.

"Alice," my mom calls behind me, her voice sharp. "You're NOT going anywhere!"

"I *have* to," I snap, tears burning my eyes. "I *need* answers! You're not going to keep me locked up just because *you're* scared!"

She steps toward me, but I'm already halfway out the door. "You don't know what you're doing!"

I stop at the threshold. "Maybe not. But at least I'm doing *something.*"

I don't wait for her to response. The door slams shut behind me, the sound final, like something in me just broke free.

***

The drive to The Escape Room was a blur of red eyes and blurry headlights. By the time I got there, the sun had dipped behind the trees, casting everything in gold and gray.

I don't even go through the front this time. Around back, I jimmy open the side door with the same key the girl had let me borrow before. She probably forgot to ask for it back, or maybe I just *forgot* to return it. Oops.

The office is exactly how I left it. Silent. Dusty. But this time, I don't bother being careful.

I tear through the drawers, yank papers from shelves, knock over the file box I'd left untouched. There has to be something I missed. Something *real*.

That's when I saw it. Tucked between a stack of printer paper and a cracked clipboard.

A folded slip of stationary with the same address from Matt's notebook written on it. Only this time, it has something else scribbled in the corner:

P.I. Office. Retired. Cleared out in 2019. Ask him.

P.I.? Private Investigator? I sink into the chair, the paper trembling in my hand. The office… that address… Matt wasn't sneaking off to meet some stranger. It wasn't where Christina was either. He was digging. He was trying to find her.

Matt wasn't stalking anyone. My stomach twists painfully. The charges—the trespassing, the harassment—they weren't about some ex-girlfriend at all. No. He was searching. Digging. Getting too close to something his father didn't want uncovered because God forbid that man actually have to *feel* something.

Of course they buried it. Of course they called him unstable. But he wasn't broken. He was brave. And no one saw that but me.

His past? It's about getting caught breaking in so he could access private records, trespassing into places that might hold answers about his mom. And his father made it all disappear.

Not to protect Matt. To protect himself. I feel rage crawl up my spine. Matt's father knows more than he's letting on. I stand up, fist still clenched around the paper. If anyone is going to answer for what the hell was going on, it's the man who's been hiding behind a title and a clean image for far too long.

TWENTY FOUR

Another drive, another disassociation episode.
Now, just the sound of the tires crunching gravel and
the fire in my chest that refuses to die as I finally make it
across town.

Mayor Ward's house looms ahead like a shadow
over the quiet neighborhood—all brick, sharp lines, and
spotless hedges. Of course it's perfect. Of course not a
blade of grass is out of place. Because that's what he
does, right? Keeps things *clean*. Well, not tonight. I'm so
thankful Matt never brought me here.

I stomp up the front steps, fueled by too little sleep
and too much betrayal, and slam my fist against the
door.

Once.

Twice.

Three times.

Loud enough to wake the dead, or at least the man who buried everything alive.

A light flicks on upstairs. Then another. I see movement behind the curtains, then the heavy clunk of locks shifting. When the door finally cracks open, there he is. Our glorious, faithful, lying, sick, twisted, Mayor Ward. Robe. Slippers. Disgustingly composed, even now.

"Alice?" he asks, groggy, confused. "It's the middle of the night—"

"Save it," I snap, shoving the door open wider. "We need to talk. Now."

His brows shoot up in shock, but I don't wait for an invitation. I storm into the house like a hurricane, the fury rolling off me in waves.

"You want to tell me what the hell you were doing burying Matt's entire past?"

He closes the door behind me with a sigh. "Alice, this really isn't—"

"No," I cut him off. "*You don't get to say it's not the time.* You made it not the time for *years*. While your son spiraled and dug and *begged* for answers about his

167

mother — and you just stood there. Watching him fall apart."

"I was trying to protect him," he says, tone flat but defensive. "He was seventeen. Acting like a child. Breaking into city buildings, harassing old detectives. He was out of control."

"He was *grieving*," I basically growl at him. "He was desperate! And you? You were too busy keeping your damn public image polished to even be a father!"

He flinches, but I'm already pacing, waving the folded paper in my hand like a weapon. "You buried his criminal record. Wiped it clean so he could have a 'normal life'? Is that what you tell yourself at night? That you were doing him a favor?"

He swallows hard, his arms crossing over his chest. "Yes. I *was* doing him a favor. I didn't want him branded. I wanted him to go to college, get out of this town, have a future. He had potential—"

"*Bullshit!*" My voice cracks, but I keep going. "You did it for *you*. You didn't want whispers about the mayor's messed-up kid. You didn't want anyone asking questions about what happened to his mother. Because if they had, they might have found out you weren't just neglectful — you were hiding something."

His jaw clenches. "Hiding something? I didn't know anything. I *still* don't know anything!"

"Then why didn't you help him?" My voice is hoarse now, trembling with emotion. "Why didn't you *care*? He lost her, and he lost *you,* too. You shut down. You left him alone. And now—" I suck in a breath, heart pounding. "Now he's back in a hospital bed, and *you're* still pretending like all of this *isn't* connected!"

He doesn't respond for a moment. Just looks down at the polished floor, as if it might give him the answers he's spent years avoiding.

Finally, he says quietly, "I didn't know how to help him. She left, and I... I couldn't look at him without seeing her. It was easier to just... make it all go away."

I shake my head, disgusted. "Well, nothing went away. You just pushed it underground. And now it's back. It's all back, and you have no idea what's been actually going on."

He lifts his gaze, something cold and unfamiliar flickering in his eyes. "What exactly are you accusing me of?"

I step closer, staring him down. "Nothing. *Yet.* But *someone* wanted Matt quiet. *Someone* is still trying to make me look crazy. And now I know for a fact — *whatever's going on didn't start with me.* It started with your *wife.* And you turned your back on all of it." My words spit like venom.

The silence between us grows. We stand there for several moments, both breathing heavily, gathering our thoughts.

Finally, he speaks, voice low and bitter, "You think you're helping him. But sometimes dragging the past into the light does more harm than good."

"Maybe," I say, walking back toward the door. "But *I'm* not afraid of the truth. And I think Matt's mother would've wanted someone to be brave enough to find it."

"Alice, wait…"

I slam the door on my way out. I can't listen to another second of his lies. He may want to keep convincing himself that his wife just walked away from her son, but there is obviously more to the story.

I don't even remember putting the car in drive. One second I'm tearing away from that perfectly manicured hellhole, the next I'm a block down the street, pulling over so hard the tires screech against the curb.

I throw it into park and just sit there, gripping the steering wheel so tightly my knuckles go white. The silence swallows me whole. And then it *cracks*.

First with a single sob. Then another. Until I'm gasping, choking on air like I've been underwater for years and finally surfaced, just to drown all over again.

Tears blur everything. The windshield. The streetlights. The world. I slam my fists against the steering wheel, once, twice, over and over until the pain shoots through my arms and into my chest.

"Why?" I scream. "Why does it *always* end like this?!"

I lean forward until my forehead hits the wheel, and the weight of everything presses down — the past, the present, the not-knowing — all of it.

I don't even know who I'm talking to. God? The universe? *Myself?*

"I let them in," I whisper, voice cracking. "I let them in, and now they're gone."

Matt.

Christina.

They became my people. My world. And now everything's slipping through my fingers, just like before.

Just like the twins.

My chest caves inward as the memory hits me like a freight train.

We were *children*. My neighbors, my best friends, my everything. I spent more time in their backyard than my own. The twins, they were like magic to me. We were inseparable.

And then, one day... they were gone. Just like that. Three bodies. One man. Their father.

Everyone in town talked about it for weeks. The tragedy. The horror. But no one talked about what it did to the *rest* of us. What it did to a little girl who thought she finally had sisters. Who stood in an empty backyard and waited for girls who would never come back.

That's when I learned that loving people meant losing them. That closeness equals pain.

So I built walls. Tall ones. Barbed wire. No one in, no one out. Safe.

Until Christina.

Until Matt.

And now, here I am again… alone, terrified, and blaming myself.

"I should've known," I mutter through clenched teeth. "I should've never let myself believe I could have people again." Tears fall faster, heavier.

"I ruin everything. I *kill* everything." I know it's not true, not really, but trauma doesn't care about the truth. It cares about patterns. It cares about scars that never healed right.

I press the palms of my hands into my eyes, trying to stop the spiraling, but it's like a dam's broken inside me. Every repressed scream, every quiet night of pretending I was fine, every fake smile at the store, it's all coming out now. And I don't know how to stop it.

"I'm so tired," I whisper. "I'm tired of being afraid. Of losing people. Of feeling like it's all my fault."

The sky outside the windshield is just beginning to turn that pre-dawn gray. The kind of light that makes everything look haunted. My phone buzzes in the cupholder, but I don't even look. I just breathe. In. Out. Try to remember who I am under all the pain.

I'm Alice. And I've survived this long. Maybe...
maybe I'm not meant to survive *alone* anymore.

But first, I have to keep going. Even if I'm
breaking. Even if it hurts. I have to finish this.

For Matt.

For Christina.

For the twins.

For the version of me that still believes it might all
be worth it. The sobs eventually taper into silence. My
body feels like it's made of sandbags... heavy,
waterlogged, and on the verge of collapse.

But I breathe.

And then I breathe again.

I reach up and wipe my cheeks with the sleeves of
my hoodie, catching the tears that refuse to stop
entirely. My hands tremble, my chest still shudders
between gulps of air.

I'm still here.

And that means I can still fight.

I lean back against the headrest and stare at the
pale, breaking sky through the windshield. It looks
washed-out and distant, but it's new. A new day. A new

chance. A flicker of something steadier settles in my chest.

"I'm not done," I whisper to the emptiness. "You *don't* get to take them from me."

My phone buzzes in the cupholder again, breaking the silence. I blink, startled, then reach for it with unsteady fingers. Matt.

"They gave me my phone and cut back the pain meds. We really need to talk. "

My breath catches in my throat again, but this time for a different reason. I reread the message, heart pounding. He's awake. He's clear. He remembers *something*.

I grip the phone in both hands, staring at the words, and a small ember of hope sparks in my chest.

Everything's not okay. But it's not over. Not yet. I start the engine.

And drive.

TWENTY FIVE

The sun is fully high in the sky once I pull into my own driveway. My eyes are burning. Head throbbing. The second I step inside, the quiet weight of the house settles over me. The hum of the porch light turning off with the sun feels heavy somehow.

I'm still wearing my pajamas that I had changed into right before the detective and that officer showed up on my porch. I forgot I was even wearing them until I caught a glimpse of myself in the hallway mirror. Comfy sweats, and an oversized, wrinkled, tear stained t-shirt.

I peel them off with trembling, tired hands and crumble them in a ball as I'm walking to my laundry room. I find some clean clothes, anything normal. Anything that helps me pretend that I'm not falling apart.

The soft creak of my floorboards announces my presence before I reach the living room. Mom stirs on the couch, and her eyes snap open. She sits up, clutching the blanket around her like a shield.

"Alice," she says softly but with steel beneath it, "where have you been? What's going on?"

I want to tell her everything all at once, but the words rush out jagged and fast. "Mom, you have to listen… there's more to Matt's past than anyone's been telling us. Mayor Ward, his wife, all of it… it's all buried and twisted."

She shakes her head, cutting me off before I can go any further. "No. Not again. You have to stop. I'm not losing you. I won't. Not after everything we have been through."

I grit my teeth, voice rising. "You lost me the day you and dad shut down after what happened to the twins. You left me to drown in silence and grief, and I was the one who had to survive it. Don't you dare sit here and speak about losing me when you walked away first! I was just a kid!"

Her voice cracks, but she keeps fighting back. "I was scared, Alice! Scared to face it all! I lost a friend too!

Their mother was a good friend. A kind friend. Do you have any idea how much guilt I carry?!"

"You don't get to do that! You treat me as if I'm already gone!" I snap. "I'm here, mom! I'm still here, and I'm done hiding! I'm not letting this lie go, Matt's story deserves to be brought to the light and told!"

She reaches out as if to touch me, then pulls back. "I just want to protect you."

"And I need you to stand *with* me instead of trying to *shield* me from it," I say, voice shaking but fierce. "I can't do this alone!"

We stare at each other, both breathing hard, both furious and scared… both desperately wanting to bridge the distance between us that has grown. This is the rawest emotion I have seen out of this woman since I was a child.

She swallows hard, eyes glistening as the fight finally drains out of her. She finally lets her hands fall to her lap, voice barely above a whisper.

"I'm sorry, Alice. I'm sorry I wasn't there for you. After the twins, I was so lost in my own grief, I forgot how to be your mother. And that's on me."

I take a shaky breath, the tension in my chest is loosening just a bit. "I needed you. I still need you."

She nods slowly, tears slipping down her cheeks. "I know. And I want to be here now. No more shutting down. No more walking away. That goes for both of us."

For a moment, all the anger fades between us, replaced by something fragile and real.

"I'm scared, Alice," she admits. "But it's time I stop letting that stop me from fighting for you... for Matt."

I reach out and finally take her hand. "We're in this together, Mom. No more silence. You have to trust me."

She squeezes my hand, a promise between us. "No more silence."

I squeeze her hand one more time, then gently pull away. "I have to make a call."

Mom nods, wiping at her face with the edge of her blanket. "Okay, I'll make some coffee."

I leave her on the couch and head out the door to the front porch. The morning bird songs ease my tension a bit. My phone is already in my hand, and my thumb hovers for a second over the contact.

179

I press Call.

It rings once. Twice.

"Alice," Claire answers, voice too clear and steady for how early it is. "I was planning on calling you later this morning. Is everything alright?"

"Yeah… I mean no, not really, but I'm okay. Matt texted me."

There's a brief pause on the other end. "He's awake?"

"Awake. Coherent. Said they gave him his phone and cut back his pain meds. He wants to talk."

"That's huge, Alice. That's really good. What are you thinking?"

"I want to go see him. Now. Before someone else gets to him first. Before anyone has a chance to manipulate his memory or push him to say something that isn't true."

"I agree. You're smart to move fast. I was informed of his past charges though, I was told you have been made aware of those?"

"Yes, I have." I pace the length of my porch back and forth. "We need to talk strategy before I go talk to him. I found out things last night. About his dad. About his mother's disappearance. I think it's all connected."

"Yeah. Half an hour? The coffee shop." I know she's being paid to be on my side, but I also believe she genuinely does have my back.

"I'll be there," she says, no hesitation. "Bring whatever you have. We'll figure out our strategy."

"Perfect, thank you."

"No, thank you, Alice. You're doing something most people wouldn't have the nerve to. Standing up to the biggest bully in this town, Mayor Ward."

We hang up, and I slowly walk back into the house. I sit down and let myself breathe, deep and slow. Mom steps into the room with two mugs, hands me one without a word.

I take it. Sip. Burn my tongue. Good. I'm awake now.

"I'm meeting Claire," I say, setting the mug down. "Then I'm going to the hospital."

She nods. No arguments this time. Just a quiet, steady kind of support. It's enough. I grab my jacket, my keys, and slide my phone into my pocket.

A burnt tongue, mission, and some resolve to my mommy issues. What a way to start the day.

Time to move.

TWENTY SIX

The coffee shop is too quiet. The kind of quiet that only exists early in the morning before the espresso machines have had time to scream. I slide into a corner booth, fingers wrapped around a scalding to-go cup. My tongue is already tender from this morning's poor decision, and now I'm burning it again. Perfect.

Claire, is already here. She doesn't do late. She's got a folder open and that no-nonsense expression I've forced myself to rely on. She glances up over her red-rimmed glasses.

"Rough morning?"

I shrug. "My mom finally stopped trying to wrap me in bubble wrap, so… progress."

Claire nods in approval, then taps the folder. "What do you have?"

I pull Matt's notebook out of my bag, still crammed with receipts and messy notes, and lay it on the table like it might bite. I haven't opened it since the other night. Just knowing it exists on my person without his permission makes my stomach twist.

"There's something going on, Claire. Something deep. Matt wasn't just spiraling, he was looking for something. About his mom."

She starts flipping through the pages. I cringe. Her brows pinch slightly. "His handwriting's a mess."

"Organized chaos," I mutter. "It starts off just about work but then he starts documenting things. He tracked people, dates, conversations... He believed her disappearance wasn't random. He believed that she didn't just walk away from him. That there were holes in the story."

"Was he chasing a theory or a person?"

I hesitate. "Maybe both. I haven't gotten far in it, only to the part with that address. It took me to an office in the next town over. I then found the same address on a separate paper, and it was for a Private Investigator. He paid a lot of money to chase just a theory."

She puts her hand up and motions to hold on. She's reading, intensely.

"Did he ever mention a journal? His mother's journal?"

"No." More secrets.

"It says in here that he found something, Alice. A red notebook. He thought it was hers. He wrote that he never opened it. He wasn't ready." Her eyes are sharp now, looking at mine.

"Does it say where he found it?" I ask.

"Not exactly, just that it was in the garage." She skims through a few more pages and closes Matt's notebook gently. "You need to try to find it. There has to be something helpful in that thing because there's nothing else we can use here."

I nod slowly.

"It's probably still at his house. His dad doesn't touch a thing. I can check today. I'll have Matt call him and get him to the hospital. I won't tell him why, he would never let me do this."

Claire watches me for a moment. "What's your gut telling you?"

"That someone knows exactly what happened to his mom. That she didn't just leave, and that there's more to the story."

Her eyebrows lift slightly. "Then go find that journal."

I leave the coffee shop with my fingers wrapped too tightly around my to-go cup, it reminds me of the one in my trashcan not too long ago.

I shudder.

***

My drive is nothing but silence and my muscle memory taking me back to Matt's house for the second time in 12 hours.

His father's car isn't in the driveway. Good. I park along the side so no one will see my car from the road and walk the rest of the way to the garage like I'm sneaking up on something that might run.

Last night was my first time in the house, but I've been inside this garage many times. Mainly whenever Matt needed to work on his truck and wanted me to keep him company.

It always smells like sawdust and insulation and the kind of cold that sinks into your skin and stays there.

The door groans when I push it open.

I flinch.

Inside, it's dim... just a small amount of light spilling through the dusty windows and single pull chain hanging from the ceiling like a noose. I pull it, and the bulb flickers on above me, then settles into a humming glow that shows the dust in the air. It doesn't help any with the shadows.

Boxes are stacked everywhere. Most are not labeled and are made of cardboard with sags in the corners from moisture. There are old campaign signs, yard tools, and fishing gear that I've never seen move from that spot. Everything smells like time and mold.

I pick a starting point and get to work. I don't know how much time I have.

Dust sticks to the sweat on my skin as I pull boxes off shelves, stack them behind me, and crack them open one by one. I find a lot of campaign flyers from over the years from his dad. An entire box of tangled extension cords. Even a dented thermos that, didn't make it to the trash.

The anxiety of not knowing if someone will find me in here keeps me moving. I make sure to be careful and place the boxes back as close to as they were. Let's hope my memory is not failing me.

I find a bin on the back of the next shelf I'm going through. It's heavier than the others, plastic instead of cardboard, lid warped slightly from something heavy pressing on it too long.

I pop it open.

Papers. Files. Stacks of bills. Receipts. A yellow envelope with handwriting I don't recognize. My hands start to tremble as I read the dates on these papers and dig deeper.

And there, at the very bottom, is a red leather notebook.

I don't move. For a second, I just stare at it, like if I reach for it, it'll vanish or bite me.

It's smaller than I imagined. Plain. Worn at the edges. The elastic band meant to hold it shut is stretched too thin and fraying.

I kneel and gently lift it out, carefully like I'm holding a new born baby.

My hands are shaking and suddenly very cold. I don't want to open it here. Not in this frozen graveyard of memories. I glance at the door and back at the notebook in my hands.

I carefully slip it into my bag and breathe. Then I start to put everything back the way I found it. As I set the tub back on the shelf, I hear the worst noise a person in my position wants to hear right now, a car door.

Oh no. No, no. There's no way he's home already.

My heart starts to beat in my throat and I feel like I might throw up right here on a box of old newspapers. I rush to grab my bag and as gently as my shaking hands will allow me, I pull on the chain and turn off the light.

I slowly push the door open, it creaks loudly and I wince. I stop and peek out the open space I've created.

Oh, thank God. I finally breathe and walk out of the garage.

Just the mailman. I could kiss him.

I don't think my heart can take much more of these high stress moments I'm putting it through.

I made it to my car.

I text Claire one word,

"Found. "

And drive like the truth is burning a hole in my passenger seat.

TWENTY SEVEN

Claire texts me just as I'm pulling into my driveway.

"Got pulled into a last-minute client meeting. Should be about an hour. I'll call when I'm done. So sorry, Alice. Talk soon."

I stare at the message for a second, thumb hovering over my screen, before sighing and killing the engine. I shouldn't be annoyed, it's not like I didn't just ask her to help me investigate a missing person's cold case using half a notebook and a hunch, but still. Timing sucks and I haven't slept.

The red leather journal is still in my bag. Heavy. Breathing. Waiting.

Inside, the house is quiet. Too quiet. My mom's out getting groceries and such. Which means I have the whole place to myself, just me and the ghosts I keep collecting.

I set my bag on the kitchen table and pace for a few minutes, back and forth between the sink and fridge like it's going to help me think.

Should I wait for Claire? What if I miss something important by trying to read this on my own? What if there's something in there I can't unsee?

I stare at my bag like it will make the decision for me.

But I already know I'm not going to wait. So, I make a cup of coffee, as if I need any more caffeine in my system.

I take the journal into my living room and sit crisscross on my couch. I pull a blanket onto my lap and let the smell of old pages hit me like a memory. It's faint, but warm. I inhale and recognize the scent of vanilla perfume, dust and something I can't name.

I pull the elastic band loose. The spine creaks. My hands are sweating and I instantly regret letting my fingers touch this thing without gloves on. The cops did not need another piece of evidence with my prints on it. I blame my tiredness for this mistake.

The first page is dated, Matt's fourth birthday.

March 3rd

He woke up earlier than usual and wanted waffles. He asked for them "the way dad makes them," but I don't think he realizes I'm the one who always gets them just right. He told me he loved me, then asked if pirates were real. I said maybe. He smiled like he'd just caught me lying.

I blink and turn the page.

March 4th

He likes when I sing to him. Even when I forget the words and start humming. He says it helps his "thoughts be quiet." He doesn't have many friends yet. The other boys don't like that he collects bugs. I told him they're wrong. Bugs are cool. He smiled again.

Page after page. Daily entries. A mother watching her son grow up, little things no one else would notice. The way he held his spoon. The way he lined up his toy trucks in color order. The time he cried when a spider drowned in the garden hose runoff.

I don't know what I expected. Not this.

I keep flipping.

March 19th

He asked if dad was mad at us again. I told him no. I lied. He knows. He uses his fingers and turns my lips and says, "smile on."

March 23rd

He covered his ears when we fought. I found him under the table and he wouldn't come out until I sang. I told him it wasn't his fault. I don't think he believes me.

My stomach clenches. There's no evidence here. No dark confession. Just grief. A woman writing to survive. To remember. To make it feel like she still had control over something.

I let out a long breath and lean back into the couch. Disappointment settles in like a fog. Nothing about where she went or a plan to leave. Nothing about being taken. Nothing at all. Just Matt, Matt, Matt.

I sip my coffee and flip another page. I have to read it all. This one is dated weeks later, no specific day, just *April* scribbled at the top like she was trying to be fast.

April

I had a dream. It was so real. I had a daughter. It was so real I woke up reaching for her.

I sit up straighter, intrigued, this is the first entry not about Matt from the get-go.

She had these stormy gray eyes and a laugh that always sounded like it was about to turn into a scream. Wild blonde hair that I could never brush down, like mine. She loved to climb. Everything. She'd fall and never cry, just to get up and try again. Stubborn. Brave. Smart in a way that scared me.

She'd talk too much when she was tired. Make up songs while brushing her teeth. Insist on three bedtime stories even when she could barely keep her eyes open. She wouldn't be quiet. Not for anyone. Not even the dark.

My hands are trembling now. Something in the back of my throat is burning.

If I ever do have my girl, I will name her after my sweet, childhood best friend.

Christina.

She will be my crazy Christina.

I reread that last line three times, this has to be sleep deprivation.

She will be my crazy Christina.

It's not a coincidence. Not a memory glitch. Not something I'm imagining. She didn't make up the name, she was given it.

Chris.

I close the notebook slowly and set it on the coffee table in front of me.

All this time, I thought I was chasing a ghost.

But I wasn't.

I was making friends with one.

TWENTY EIGHT

I pace the living room for ten minutes before I can bring myself to call Claire. She answers on the second ring.

"Tell me you found something," she says, no greeting, no pretense.

"I did." My voice is tight. My hands are still cold. "I found the red notebook. Matt's mom's."

Silence on the line. Not the kind that says she doesn't believe me, but the kind that says she does.

"Coffee shop," Claire says. "Now."

Twenty minutes later, I'm sliding the journal across the table like it's radioactive. Claire flips it open carefully. Her fingers are light, reverent, like she's afraid the pages might crack. She reads in silence, pausing only once to glance up at me.

"She was keeping track of him," she murmurs. "Every little thing. Daily details. Patterns. Emotional cues."

"She was trying to hold on," I say quietly. "To Matt. To herself."

Claire nods once and flips further, eyes scanning. I know the exact page she lands on. I know because her shoulders go still and her eyes narrow just slightly.

She reads the entry about the daughter. The wild hair. The stubborn laugh. The name.

"If I ever do have my girl, I will name her after my sweet, childhood best friend. Christina."

Claire leans back in her chair, eyes still on the page. I don't say anything. I don't have to. After a few seconds, she closes the journal and folds her hands together.

"Christina."

"Chris," I confirm. "The girl I've been calling my best friend."

Claire exhales slowly. "She's his sister." She says through her breath.

"I think so," I whisper. "Pregnant when she disappeared? Or… Half-sister, maybe? Same mom, different dad? Born after she disappeared."

Claire's silent again, but this time it's the kind where her brain is moving a mile a minute. She pulls her laptop over, opens a document, and starts typing. Her fingers are fast and sharp. Government databases, local records, anything she can access with a few keystrokes and the right login credentials.

She checks birth certificates. Hospital records. School enrollments. Employment history.

I sit there in the silence, almost finishing my coffee, the scream of the espresso machine filling the room like static.

Then she stops.

Stares at the screen.

And says, "She doesn't exist."

My stomach drops. "What do you mean?"

"I mean there is no Christina born to Matt's mother. There's no Christina born in this county that fits that age range. No matching social security number. No driver's license. No education history. No voter registration."

I lean forward. "She worked at the store. With me. She had a schedule, a paycheck. She paid rent."

Claire looks at me sharply. "Then someone either gave her a fake identity... or looked the other way."

"But it's a locally owned grocery store," I say. "It's not some faceless company. They don't do real background checks."

"They might not," Claire says, "but they still need tax info. Even small businesses file W-2s. Which means either she used stolen information… or someone inside helped her fake it."

A chill creeps up my spine.

Someone helped her.

"Who?" I ask softly. "Who would help someone like that hide in plain sight?"

Claire shuts the laptop. "That's the question, isn't it?"

My thoughts are spiraling. Chris, Christina, never really talked about her past. She was always good at deflecting. Laughing things off. Never going too deep. And I never pushed. Because I trusted her.

Stupid. Stupid, stupid.

"What do I do now?" I ask.

Claire's voice is calm. Controlled. "You talk to Matt. Carefully. If what you found is true... he has a sister he never knew about. And she's been in your lives for months, maybe even longer. And Alice—"

"Yeah?"

"Don't go anywhere alone." She shuts her laptop and leans back in her chair, folding her arms tightly like she's trying to hold something inside. Her eyes stay fixed on the journal between us.

"She's a ghost," she says, voice low. "And ghosts don't pass background checks. Someone helped her, Alice. Someone wanted her here."

I don't answer. I'm not sure I have words left.

The silence stretches between us, thick with unspoken questions and the weight of what we've just learned.

I shift in the booth, dragging my knees up toward my chest. The cushions are soft, worn down from hours of caffeine filled conversations. The Brew Crew is warm, and suddenly my body remembers how long it's been since I slept.

She keeps talking, mostly to herself now, half-muttered thoughts about social security fraud, forged

IDs, local connections, but her voice fades into the background. Like white noise. Distant thunder.

I blink slowly, staring at the journal on the table. The red leather cover. The frayed elastic band.

She will be my crazy Christina.

My eyes burn.

I lean my head on the window and watch the countless cars go by. Just for a second. I just need to rest my eyes.

My heartbeat slows. The weight of everything sinks into my chest like sand.

I try to hold on to the thoughts, the questions, the urgency, the plan to call Matt, but they slip like water through my fingers.

I dream of a hallway lined with mirrors. Each one shows a different version of Chris.

Laughing.

Crying.

Bleeding.

Smiling.

I ask her which one is real. She just tilts her head and draws a smiley face on the glass between us.

I wake with a jolt to the sound of the screaming, over-used, espresso machine. Then, Claire's voice and the dull buzz of her phone. She answers it briskly, not even looking my way.

I sit up slowly, heart pounding, the dream already unraveling.

She hangs up, turns to me, and says, "He's awake. If you're going to tell him… now's probably the time."

I nod.

And this time, I don't hesitate.

TWENTY NINE

My eyes are tired. I can't remember the last time I truly slept. But I'm in the car now, and the air is cold through the cracked window. It cuts through the heat of my skin like a warning: stay awake.

Music off. Phone on silent. It's just me and the low rumble of the engine.

And my thoughts.

God, my thoughts.

I keep going back to the first day I met Chris. How easy she was to like. How she looked me right in the eyes like she'd known me forever. Like I *belonged* to her already.

She was magnetic in that quiet, warm way that made you lean in without realizing you were giving anything away.

I trusted her so quickly.

Too quickly.

I think about the day she brought me soup when I was sick. The time she cried watching a commercial and said she "wasn't used to people being so soft." The dumb nickname she had for Matt—*Golden Retriever Boy.*

She never talked about her past. Not in a vague way… more like it just didn't exist. I asked her once if she had siblings and she'd laughed, shrugged, said, "If I do, they're avoiding me as well as I avoid them."

I thought she was just being funny.

Now it feels like a warning I was too blind to hear.

I take a turn without thinking, muscle memory driving me toward the hospital. My hands are tight on the wheel, knuckles pale. I don't even try to loosen them.

What if this is all in my head?

What if I'm seeing patterns that don't exist? Grief makes people weird. Trauma makes you cling to meaning in meaningless things.

But what if it's not in my head? What if everything that I thought was safe was actually a setup?

I start to think back, really think, about how she'd act around Matt.

And I realize something.

Every single time he came around… she was gone. I thought it was coincidence.

Maybe she was just busy. Or needed alone time. Or didn't want to be a third wheel.

But now?

Now I see it for what it was. She avoided him.

Not overtly. Not suspiciously. Just enough. Disappearing right before he'd show up. Making excuses to leave. Saying she had to go check on her friend's cat, or cover a shift, or suddenly not feeling well.

Like she couldn't risk being in the same room with him too long.

Like seeing him too close might crack the mask she'd worked so hard to hold in place.

I think about how she always asked questions about him. Casual stuff, said like jokes.

"Do you think Matt would ever run for office like his dad?"

"Was he a mama's boy growing up?"

"Has he ever talked about therapy?"

I laughed. I answered. I never once stopped to think about why she wanted to know.

It's like I gave her the blueprint without realizing it. I handed her the keys to his past. To *our* lives. And she used them to dismantle us piece by piece.

Claire said *Christina doesn't exist.* But I knew her. She slept on my couch. She painted her nails at my kitchen table. She watched *Jeopardy* and ate bowls of cereal in my living room.

And now I have to look Matt in the eye and tell him:

"She's your sister. And she's been here the whole time."

The hospital sign blinks into view, and something in my chest pulls tight.

Matt's been through enough. His body's still healing. His memory is Swiss cheese. And I'm about to hand him another heart break.

I don't know what I'm walking into.

I don't know what he remembers, or if he's strong enough to face what I've found.

But I know I owe him the truth.

Even if it breaks him.

Even if it breaks me.

I park and sit there for a long minute, staring at the entrance like it might eat me whole. My fingers tap against the steering wheel—no rhythm, just nerves.

I sit still for too long. My hands are shaking and my eyes are foggy. I need sleep. This could change everything.

It probably *will*.

I grab the red notebook from the passenger seat, press it to my chest for a second like it might give me courage, and then get out of the car.

Inside the hallway smells like bleach and forced comfort. The fake peace hospitals always try to sell you. It doesn't work. My shoes squeak softly against the floor.

I pass the nurse's station, they don't look up. I pass the vending machine that never works and steals quarters. I pass the waiting room where I sat, full of anxiety, waiting to be taken back to finally see him alive. I pass the window where I watched the sun rise after sitting by his bedside all night.

Matt's door is just ahead.

Closed.

Behind it is the man I love.

Behind it is the truth that might break him.

I stand there with my hand hovering over the handle.

I can't hear anything. Not my heart. Not my breath.

The notebook is heavy in my bag.

My body feels heavier.

I force a shaky breath.

And knock.

THIRTY

The second I step inside, I lose my ability to form even a thought. I don't know how to bring this up casually without dropping the truth like a bomb.

Matt is propped up in bed, IV in one arm, a book in his lap he clearly hasn't been reading. His hair is a mess of half-dried curls, and there are still shadows under his eyes, but he looks… present. Alive in a way he didn't the last time I saw him.

His eyes land on me, and he smiles… small, tired, but real.

It almost breaks me.

"Hey," he says.

"Hey."

I walk slowly toward him. He sets the book aside and reaches out for me without thinking. Our fingers lace, and for a second, I let myself believe this might be okay. That maybe I can talk around the edges of what I came here to say. Let it leak out slowly instead of crashing into the center of his chest.

"You look better," I say, sitting down on the edge of the bed. "More color in your face."

He lifts a brow. "You mean less dead."

I try to laugh. "Sure, if you want to go there."

He shrugs, smirking a little. "Nurses keep saying I'm doing better. I still feel like I've been hit by a truck, but apparently that's progress."

"Truck is a big step up from how malnourished and dehydrated you were," I offer.

He squeezes my hand. "You been okay?"

I nod automatically, too fast. "Yeah. Just… catching up on life. Talking to my lawyer, Claire. Drinking way too many cups of coffee."

His smile fades just slightly, and his voice drops. "Why haven't I heard from you?"

I blink. "What?"

"You texted. Once. After leaving the other day. But since then… nothing. Not a visit. Not a call. Why?"

I glance down at our hands, suddenly afraid of what he'll do when I tell him. How fast that warmth between our fingers might vanish.

"I just didn't want to overwhelm you," I say. "You've been through so much. I figured I'd wait until—"

He tilts his head. "Alice."

I stop.

He knows me too well.

I swallow. "Fine, that's not the truth."

He doesn't say anything. Just waits. I take a breath that hurts going in.

"I need to tell you something. And I don't know how to start. I've been trying to figure out the right words, but I keep running into the fact that there's no version of this that's easy."

Matt's expression tightens. His body tenses a little under the blanket.

"Alice, what's going on?"

My heart starts pounding. "The other night… I went to your house."

His brow furrows. "What? Why?"

I swallow hard. "I kind of went off on your dad."

213

The reaction is instant. He sits up straighter, the shift small but jarring.

"You *what?*"

"I—I needed answers. The cops showed up at my house telling me you had done all of these things in your past and that your dad had it all buried, and I just… I needed to understand."

"You went to *my* house," he says, voice sharp now. "And talked to *him* without me."

"I know. I know I should've told you. But I wasn't thinking clearly, and—"

His hand slips out of mine. I stop talking. My skin burns where his fingers used to be. He's staring at me, eyes narrowed, hurt flickering just beneath the surface.

I sigh and close my eyes, "there's more," I whisper.

Matt leans back slightly. "Of course there is."

"I also went into your office."

His breath catches.

"I found a journal. The one with your notes. About your mom. The private investigator. The address."

"You read it?" he asks, and his voice sounds smaller now. *Tired.* Not angry anymore, just wounded.

I nod, barely able to speak. "Yes. I shouldn't have. I had no right. But I didn't know what else to do, and I felt like the walls were closing in, and everyone was lying or missing, and… I'm sorry. I'm so sorry, Matt."

He doesn't answer. Just blinks at me in disappointment. I can't imagine how violated he feels.

I sigh again, "I didn't stop there," I admit. "Claire found something in it… About a red journal. You said you found it but couldn't bring yourself to open it."

His eyes stay locked onto mine and his cheeks turn red.

"I went to the garage, Matt."

He lets out a quick breath, "you broke into my garage? What the hell, Alice."

His voice is calm, but it cuts straight through me.

"I didn't break anything. I just went in. I searched until I found it."

He looks away.

"I hate that I did it," I say, voice cracking. "I hate that I crossed that line. You trusted me, and I went behind your back. I feel sick about it. But… Matt—"

I reach for my bag. "I found something. And you need to see it."

215

I can see his nostrils flaring and jaw line tensing even more. He is not happy with me right now and I might throw up.

I pull the red notebook out of my bag and set it on the bed by his feet. His eyes snap to it. Tears start to swell up in his eyes.

"You had no right!"

"You're right, I didn't. And I wish I could look you in the face and lie and say I regret doing what I've done, but I don't. Because I found some truth in this thing, Matt!" I point to the book. "Can you please just listen to what I have to say before you react anymore? Please?!"

He's so vulnerable right now, I'm trying so hard to remind myself why I did this.

He takes a moment, and then nods.

"Okay, good. I didn't know what I was going to find," my voice cracks, knowing what I'm about to do to him. "But it wasn't this. I never could have pictured I would find a journal full of pages and pages of how much she loved you. How much she *saw* you. How she knew what was happening around her and still did her best to protect you."

I see something break in his face. A few of the tears finally break free and are running down his cheeks.

"This entire book is full of daily details that she loved about you, Matt. Except for one entry. Would you like to read it yourself? Or I can read it to you."

"I don't think I can bear to hold that thing, just read it." His voice shakes.

"That's fine." I pick up the leather time capsule and gently turn through the pages until I land on the one I need. My stomach turns when I see her name again.

I clear my throat, read the page, and stop right before the part that I know will change everything for him. I glance up and see his face soft, dreaming with his mother about a sister he never knew.

"Okay... If I ever do have my girl, I will name her after my sweet, beloved, grandmother." I pause again to try to calm myself. I really might throw up. "Christina... She will be my crazy Christina."

Everything feels frozen.

His voice is barely there. "Christina?"

I nod. "Yes. And she's not just a dream your mom had one night. I think she's real. I think... I think she's

217

been here the whole time. Watching. Following. Manipulating everything."

He blinks several times. "What are you saying?"

I feel frustrated that he's not connecting the dots like I did. But I remind myself of his current state, and the fact that Chris did always avoid him.

"Matt… My friend, Chris, I think she's your sister."

He takes another minute to process. "So, you're telling me I spent years chasing ghosts… Begging people to talk to me. Following dead leads. Wondering if I was crazy. If she really was just gone and didn't want me. Trying to force myself to just accept it."

I stay quiet and let him feel his way through this.

"And you found all of this," he says, not looking at me. "You found the biggest connection to my mom is less than a week?!"

His eyes are wide. Determined and burning. I remain quiet, not sure how to respond.

"Has Chris been found yet?" He asks sharply.

I shake my head.

"She disappeared the same way your mom did. Car was found clean in a parking lot in the next town over," I say. "No one's seen her since."

Matt leans back against the pillows, his jaw working. I can see the gears turning. Hurt, confusion, fury… and something colder.

"She's not running," he says quietly. "She's waiting."

"Waiting for what?"

"I don't know. But if she's who attacked me, I think the only reason I'm back here, is because I wouldn't wake up. She hit my head too hard and I was going to starve to death if she didn't bring me back. That's the only explanation I can come up with."

I nod my head and agree. Gently grabbing his mom's book and putting it back in bag, my hand brushes something that wasn't there earlier. A small, stiff piece of paper.

I freeze.

I didn't put anything else in there.

Slowly, I pull it out.

It's a folded square of printer paper.

My name is written on the front in thick, black ink. No return address. No stamp.

Just *Alice*.

Scribbled like it was done in a rush, or in rage.

I unfold it with shaking fingers.

One line.

Hope you found what you were looking for.

I look up at Matt, throat tight. "No. She's not running," I whisper. "She's watching us."

And she wants us to know it.

THIRTY ONE

It's been three days since everything changed.

Three days since I found the journal. Since I read that name out loud and watched Matt's world crack in real time. Since the letter showed up in my bag—silent, smug, and signed with a smile.

But nothing's happened since. No new notes. No shadowed figures. No signs of Chris. Just quiet.

For the first time in what feels like weeks, I've slept more than four hours at a time. I've made actual meals. I even finished a cup of coffee before it went cold. And while none of that makes anything better, it makes it feel *possible*. Like I might be able to keep going.

Today, Matt's getting discharged from the hospital.

They wanted to keep him longer, but he pushed. Said he'd recover faster outside of those fluorescent-lit walls. I don't think that's true, but I also don't blame him. He needs space. He needs something that feels normal again, even if normal isn't on the table.

He's coming to stay with me.

Not because it's romantic, or sweet, or because he's ready to play house again. But because his father won't let me in the house, and there's no one else to make sure Matt takes care of himself.

And because deep down, I think he knows this is far from over.

I'm waiting in the discharge lobby when he comes out, slow and stiff in a gray hoodie and jeans that hang a little looser on him now. There's a healing scab above his left eyebrow and a cast on one wrist, but it's the way his eyes move that gets me.

He's sharper now. Not clearer—sharper. More focused. More on edge. He's not letting himself forget anything.

"Hey," I say as I stand up.

He gives a tired half-smile. "You bring me anything good?"

"Homemade soup and a bag of gummy worms."

"Perfect."

He leans into me just slightly as I take his bag and loop my arm through his. It's not a romantic gesture. It's practical. But there's something in the weight of him next to me that feels different. Like we've passed some invisible threshold.

Back at my house, he drops his bag in the corner of the living room and immediately sinks into the couch.

I set the soup on the stove and get two mugs of tea going, because I don't know what else to do with my hands.

"I know it's not ideal," I say carefully. "But I figured this would be better than you being alone at your dad's. Or… anywhere near him."

Matt's eyes stay on the ceiling. "He doesn't want me there anyway. Not after the cops came by. And I'm not sure I'd want to be there even if he did."

"You can stay as long as you need."

"Thanks."

A moment of quiet.

Then, he sits up. "You know we have to take it in."

I pause, mid-stir.

"The notebook," he says. "The journal. The address. The investigator. All of it. We need to take it to the police."

"I know," I say softly. "I was just waiting for you to be ready."

He rubs a hand over his face. "I don't know if I'll ever be ready. But if we wait too long…"

"She could vanish," I finish.

"She already has."

Another moment.

"I have everything organized," I tell him. "Copies of both journals. Your notes. My timeline. Claire wants to come with us when we go in."

He nods, slow and steady. "Tomorrow?"

"Tomorrow."

He leans his head back again. "Then tonight, we rest. Together."

"For the first time in a long time."

I'm grateful my mom agreed to stay at the hotel tonight.

She didn't argue. Just packed a bag, hugged me a little too tightly, and told me to call if I needed anything. I think she could feel how much I needed the house to be quiet. For him. Just to settle into the next version of normal.

Now, the lights are dim, the windows are shut, and there's an old black-and-white movie playing on the TV. Something we've both seen a dozen times but can't name without looking it up.

Matt's curled into one side of the couch, blanket around his legs, spoon dangling in his empty soup bowl. I'm next to him, not touching, but close enough to feel the shift of his breath when he laughs at the dumb line delivery from his favorite mustached detective.

It's not the same as it used to be. But it's not broken either.

It's something.

I don't press. Don't ask if he's okay. Don't bring up the journal or the hospital or the name we still haven't said out loud since that day.

For tonight, the movie is enough.

By the time the credits roll, Matt's fallen asleep with his head tilted back against the couch cushion. His mouth's slightly open, his chest rising slow and steady. The lines around his eyes have softened. The storm is quiet, at least for now.

I gently gather the bowls and mugs, rinse them in the sink, and move around the house like someone afraid to wake a baby.

I turn off the lights. I make sure the doors are locked.

Then I curl up on the other side of the couch, legs tucked under me, just watching him sleep.

It feels… safe.

Until he starts to stir.

It's subtle at first. A twitch of his fingers. A wrinkle in his brow. A soft sound, like he's arguing with someone who isn't there.

Then it builds.

His breathing changes—faster, shallow. His fingers curl into fists beneath the blanket, his lips moving without sound. I sit up, heart thudding.

"No," he whispers. "Wait—please—"

He jerks once, and I reach out to touch his shoulder. "Matt… hey. You're dreaming. It's okay."

He flinches hard, eyes flying open, but they don't see me right away. They're wide, glassy, caught between now and something else.

He's still in it.

"She said it was your fault," he whispers.

I freeze. "What?"

"She said… if I'd just tried harder… Mom would still be alive."

His voice breaks on the last word. He blinks rapidly, breath shaking.

"She was standing in the hallway. Chris. Smiling, but not like she used to. Like she knew something I didn't."

I gently take his hand. "It was just a dream."

He shakes his head. "She said I stopped looking. That I gave up. That we could've saved her. If I'd just… kept going."

There's a pause, then he adds, quieter:

"She said… *You saved yourself.*"

The words hang there, heavy and sharp. I don't know if it's what Chris would say. But I know it's what he's afraid she already believes.

I press my hand against his arm, grounding him. His skin is damp with sweat. His breath is still uneven.

"Come on," I whisper. "Let's get you upstairs."

He doesn't fight me. Doesn't say anything at all. Just lets me help him up, his movements sluggish and

227

stiff like the dream took something out of him physically, too. I guide him up the stairs one careful step at a time, holding onto him like I might lose him if I let go.

When we reach my room, I help him settle into the bed. I pull the covers up over his chest and sit on the edge for a moment, watching his eyes drift half-closed, then snap open again like he's afraid to go back under.

"I'm right here," I say. "You're not alone."

He nods, barely.

I press a hand gently to his shoulder and turn off the lamp and crawl into bed.

The sheets are cool, the room quiet. I should feel safe. I should be able to sleep. I finally got a few days of peace. I thought tonight would bring more of the same.

But now all I can hear is her voice.

You saved yourself.

I turn onto my side and stare at the wall, wide awake. Sleep won't come easy tonight.

THIRTY TWO

The police station looks small this early in the morning. Empty. Like it hasn't woken up yet. But my stomach is already twisting. I hate this building. I hate the echo in the hallway, the buzz of the fluorescents, the way the walls feel like they're listening.

I glance over at Matt.

He looks worse than he did when I picked him up. His shoulders are slumped, eyes half-lidded, jaw clenched like he hasn't breathed in ten minutes. Neither of us slept last night, not really. He tossed and turned and mumbled things I couldn't quite make out. Guilt. Names. Pleas that made no sense.

A car pulls in beside us.

Claire steps out, sharp and put-together as always, black coat flapping in the breeze like she's about to walk into a courtroom instead of a town police station. She spots us, gives a small nod, and meets us at the entrance.

"You two holding up okay?" she asks softly.

Matt doesn't answer. I just nod once.

We're escorted back to that same meeting room as before, the one I've started to loathe with every cell in my body. Same walls. Same humming light above. Same table that looks like it's been wiped clean too many times but never feels clean enough.

Detective Harper walks in with a manila folder under one arm and a half-empty coffee in the other.

He smiles like we're old friends. "You again. You know, if you insist on doing my job for me, we're gonna have to get you your own parking spot, Alice."

Claire chuckles softly. I even let out a half-laugh. But when I glance at Matt, he's staring down at the table. Still. Like the wood grain is the only thing tethering him to the earth.

Claire notices as well and clears her throat gently, refocusing the room.

"Alice," she says, turning toward me, "Did you bring everything we discussed?"

I nod, unzipping the folder in my lap. "Yeah. Everything's in here."

I slide it across the table. Detective Harper catches it, flipping it open. His brow lifts slightly as he scans the pages.

He whistles. "Well, this is thorough. Timeline, evidence logs, copies of journal entries, even the contact info for the PI?"

Claire nods. "Some of that was mine."

He glances between us. "Either of you ever thought about applying to the academy?"

"I'd rather not have to deal with someone like me every day," I mutter.

That earns a small smirk from Harper as he continues flipping through the file.

"What you've put together here, well, this isn't amateur," he says, tapping a few of the pages. "This is the kind of file that makes people uncomfortable. Because it's detailed. It's emotional. It's not built for plausible deniability."

He looks up at me. "I'll be honest, Alice. This is impressive."

I sit up straighter, tension tightening in my neck.

"But not surprising," he adds. "If anyone was going to take the investigation into their own hands around here, it was gonna be you."

He turns toward Matt. "You have anything to add?"

Matt doesn't move.

"Matthew? Anything to add?" the detective says again, slightly louder.

Still nothing.

I gently reach out and rest my hand on his shoulder.

He jolts, eyes flying up. "Sorry. What?"

Harper softens, his voice lowering. "Didn't mean to startle you. Just asking if there's anything else we should know. Anything you remember. Conversations, moments. Even if they felt small at the time."

Matt opens his mouth, closes it again. Then he says, "I… I don't know. There were little things. Chris was always around Alice. Always friendly at the grocery store. But she'd disappear when my name came up. I didn't think anything of it back then. I just thought maybe she was shy."

His hands fidget in his lap. "I never would've guessed…"

He's gone again.

Harper nods, thoughtful. "That's the thing about people like her. They count on you not guessing."

A silence falls across the table.

"Just so you know," the detective says gently, "I believe you. All of you. And I take this seriously."

Claire crosses her arms. "Then you understand why we're here. She may not exist on paper, but she's no ghost, Detective. She's a very real threat."

"Oh, I know she is," he says. "I've already requested a case review. I'm going to run this against cold case files, missing persons logs, the PI records. I'll need time. But I'll find her."

He stands, tucking the folder under his arm. "I'm going to get this submitted into evidence, bring the rest of my team up to speed, and begin my search for your not-ghost."

He pauses at the door, eyes landing on Matt one last time. His eyes soft.

"In the meantime, I'll add extra patrols in both your neighborhoods. As a precaution. Just in case she's closer than we think."

We gather our belongings and head back to the parking lot.

I help Matt into the passenger seat, buckle him in gently. He doesn't say much, just closes his eyes like the world is too bright. I close the door, exhaling as I move to walk around the front of the car.

That's when I see her.

Across the street.

Sitting on a bench by the courthouse steps, legs crossed, hands folded in her lap.

That hair. Those slouched shoulders. And that hoodie.

Chris's hoodie.

My mouth goes dry. I'd know it anywhere. Oversized, black, frayed around the cuffs. But it's not just that. There's a stain just under the collar. I remember exactly how it got there. Chris spilled spaghetti sauce on it the night we binge-watched horror movies and laughed until we cried.

That hoodie lived at my house for weeks. My pulse slams into my throat.

Claire's already unlocking her own car, so I call out, "Claire! Can you stay with Matt for a sec?"

She looks up, brows furrowed. "Of course."

I don't wait. I move fast, anger sparking with every step. I'm done. I didn't sleep. I watched him flinch through nightmares all night. And now she's here, sitting in plain sight like it's a joke?

"Chris!" I shout.

The girl doesn't move.

"Hey!" I yell louder, charging across the street. "You think this is funny? You think haunting him like this is some kind of game?!"

I'm feet away now. I can see the hoodie more clearly… the faded fabric, the tiny burn hole near the hem, the way it hangs like it was made for someone taller.

She finally looks up.

And she's not Chris.

She's younger. Pale, startled, earbuds still dangling from one ear. She looks like she was just waiting for a bus. Confused. Scared.

"Uh… sorry?" she says, leaning back slightly.

I stop cold, heart pounding. "Where the hell did you get that hoodie?"

She blinks, looks down at herself like she forgot what she was wearing.

"I dunno. Some girl gave it to me."

I stare at her.

"She gave me five bucks and told me to sit here for a while wearing it," she says, like it's no big deal. "Said it was for some… social media project or something?"

My stomach twists.

Claire is beside me now, silent and wide-eyed.

I look back across the street at Matt in the passenger seat.

He's watching me through the window.

But I don't think he's surprised.

I think he already knew.

THIRTY THREE

It's been three weeks.

No notes. No sightings. No more strange faces in familiar places. Just quiet. Long, uneasy quiet.

The extra patrols the department put in place have started thinning out. I still see a cruiser roll through the neighborhood every other night, but the presence isn't heavy like it was. I think they're starting to believe it's over. That we scared her off. But I don't think that.

I think she's just waiting.

My mom finally went home last week. It wasn't a tearful goodbye. More like an exhausted hug and a reminder to call if I so much as sneeze. Although, she still calls three times a day, minimum. Morning, afternoon, and just before bed. I don't blame her. But I can't keep living in that kind of fear. I've already had the locks changed twice, and a new alarm system put on every window and door.

Still, I double-check the bolt every night. Sometimes more than once.

Matt's staying quiet.

He's been helping around the house more, making himself useful. It's his way of staying distracted. We don't talk about the dreams anymore. Not since that night he told me what she said. I don't ask if they've stopped.

I don't think they have.

His father has only called once. Said he didn't want anything to do with the case. Told Matt, "It's just too hard son, let it go." Said the past was in the past, and dragging up old ghosts was a waste of energy.

Matt didn't argue. He just hung up.

Detective Harper calls occasionally. Not often. Just enough to keep me tethered to the case like a string tied around my ribs.

One call was about a case in a smaller town about an hour from here. A break-in at a gas station. No money taken, just food, pads, tampons. Essentials.

Description matched Chris.

Another call was about a cold case from nearly six months ago, a stolen car abandoned in the woods outside the town. They found some of the items that were stolen from that gas station.

Two different counties. Two different stories. One ghost.

Harper said no one connected the dots before because the crimes were too minor. No one thought to look across jurisdiction lines. But now they're seeing the pattern. A trail. A quiet drift of desperation masked as survival.

She's been here.

She's *always* been here.

The last call was just this morning. He sounded tired. More human than usual.

Apparently, the grocery store manager finally admitted something he should've said weeks ago.

Chris showed up a few months back, said she was escaping an abusive marriage from another state. Said she left with nothing but the clothes on her back. No phone. No ID. Just a bruised face and a sweet, soft voice.

Eye roll.

The manager said he felt sorry for her. Gave her a job under the table while she got on her feet. Paid her in cash. No questions asked.

Harper said they're trying to trace her now, but it's like chasing wind. She's not just hiding… she's fully living the lie.

I pull into the grocery store parking lot ten minutes before my shift.

The weathers finally cooled down, crisp enough that I have to zip my hoodie and keep both hands in my pockets.

The store looks the same. It always looks the same. And somehow that makes it worse. Like the world just kept spinning while everything underneath it fractured.

I nod to the girl working the front as I walk past, head toward the employee room. The hall is empty.

I push the door open and step inside. It smells like old lockers and generic body spray. My locker's near the end of the row. I twist the handle and pull it open, expecting to find my bag, my water bottle, my shift badge.

Instead, I see a jar.

Glass. Heavy. Sitting perfectly centered on the top shelf.

Same brand as always. Same slightly dented lid. Same ugly label.

Alfredo sauce.

My breath catches before I even fully process what I'm looking at. I reach up slowly, hands already shaking.

Please don't be there. Please. Please. PLEASE don't be there.

With my eyes shut tight, I turn the jar over.

Dammit.

THIRTY FOUR

I force myself to set it down gently back on the shelf, like it's glass-thin and full of poison. Which, in a way, it is.

Why the Alfredo sauce?

The message. The smiley face. The timing. The knowledge that she's still here, still watching, still *ten steps ahead.*

I stare at it.

It stares back.

How did she get in? This store has cameras. Regular foot traffic. Employees. Deliveries. *People.* And no one saw a thing. Not even with her face plastered all over town? Flyers are on every store window, cork boards, gas station doors. A hand-drawn sketch in every break room within a fifty-mile radius.

And she still got in.

Right past them. Right past me.

My breath stutters in my throat. My hands are sweating. My vision narrows to a point so small it feels like I might just *shut off*.

I close the locker. Lean my forehead against the cool metal.

Do I call the detective? Tell him she was *here*, in the building, in my space?

Do I call Matt? Tell him she slipped past both of us… again?

My fingers hover over my phone, heart pounding, every instinct screaming *do something.*

But then I hear her voice in my head. Sweet. Sad. Twisted.

"You're always so easy to rattle."

No.

Not this time.

I don't want to give her the satisfaction. I don't want to feed whatever game she's playing.

If I call Harper, they'll comb the security footage, and they won't find her. She'll be a blur or a ghost or somehow just… gone. Again.

And Matt? Matt will spiral. He's barely slept in days. I won't put this on him. Not now. Not until it matters.

That's enough.

I open the locker again, grab the jar, and hold it tight like I'm holding a grenade with the pin still in place.

I walk to the back, past the mop sink, past the breaker panel, out the back door and toss it straight into the dumpster without looking twice.

The clang of glass hitting metal echoes louder than it should.

Like the sound of me *deciding* something.

I go back to my locker, slam it shut, and take a slow breath in. Let it out.

She wants me scared. She wants me shaken.

So I won't give her that.

Not today.

***

I finish my shift with my head held high. I smile at customers. I restock shelves. I even laugh with one of the new girls who tried to lift a case of water and almost fell backwards. I let the manager thank me for picking up extra hours like I didn't find a message from a ghost in my locker an hour earlier.

Because I'm done letting her control the way I breathe.

By the time I get home, the sun's starting to slip past the horizon, painting everything in gold and lavender. It's the kind of quiet that used to scare me, back when I thought silence meant something was about to go wrong.

But not tonight.

Tonight, it feels like mine.

Matt's on the couch with a blanket over his legs and his laptop open in front of him. The house smells like garlic and basil and something warm. He looks up when he hears the door and smiles without thinking.

"You cooked?" I ask, kicking off my shoes.

"I did," He says, sitting up straighter. "Don't get used to it." He chuckles, and I grab two plates from the kitchen.

"I made pasta." I freeze for a split second. Of course he made pasta.

No. She doesn't get to win.

I'm not afraid of symbols anymore. I'm reclaiming dinner, too.

I set his plate in front of him and curl up on the arm of the couch with mine.

He takes a bite and groans. "Okay, this is definitely better than hospital food."

"I mean, that's a low bar."

We eat for a minute in silence before I launch into a story from work, about the toddler who screamed the whole way through the checkout line, and how the dad just stood there nodding while she wailed like a siren.

Matt laughs, really laughs, and the sound settles something deep in my chest.

"You seem different," he says after a minute. "Lighter."

I nod, wiping sauce off my lip. "I am."

He watches me carefully.

"I threw the jar away," I say. "The one she left in my locker."

His brow tightens. "Wait—what?"

"She was at the store," I explain. "Left a jar of Alfredo with a smiley face. Same as the first time. Same brand. Same message."

His smile fades.

"But I didn't call the detective," I add before he can spiral. "Didn't tell anyone. Just threw it out. Because I'm done, Matt. I'm done playing her game. I'm done being afraid of shadows."

He sits very still.

"I want my life back," I say. "Our life. I want us to move forward. To stop waiting for her next move like she's the one in charge."

Matt's eyes glisten, but he doesn't blink.

"You should move the rest of your things here," I say. "Make this place ours. A real home."

He swallows hard, then nods. "Yeah. Yeah, I'd like that."

Later, we're curled up on the couch again, the TV playing quietly in the background. The dishes are in the sink. The lights are low. For once, the quiet isn't threatening.

Matt shifts beside me and glances over, that lazy half-smile back on his face. "You ever think about taking a trip? Just… disappearing for a little while?" He slightly winces at his own choice of words.

I turn my head toward him. "Like… pack up and go full witness protection?"

He chuckles. "No, not like that. I mean something normal. Vacation-normal. Just us. Somewhere quiet. No past. No ghosts. No surprise notes in strange places."

I raise an eyebrow. "You want a beach? Mountains? Or the classic middle-of-nowhere cabin horror movie setup?"

He laughs, softer now. "Anywhere that doesn't smell like antiseptic or emotional trauma."

I smile and lean my head against his shoulder. "I wouldn't mind a beach. Somewhere warm. Somewhere I can wear sandals and not carry pepper spray in my pocket."

He shifts a little closer. "Or we could drive up and see your parents. Just for a weekend. You've been saying you wanted to."

I blink. "You'd actually do that?"

"Sure. I mean, I'll have to survive your mom's protective death stares, but... I think I could handle it."

I laugh, like *really* laugh. It comes from somewhere deep, somewhere that hasn't had a chance to breathe in a long time. "That's brave of you."

"I'm feeling bold tonight," he says. Then, quieter: "Being around you… when you're like this. Focused. Certain. It makes everything feel less *heavy*."

I take his hand.

"Then let's go somewhere. Beach or parents or a dingy little motel halfway to nowhere. I don't care. I just want to feel like we're moving forward."

He nods. "Yeah. Let's do it. Let's start planning."

There's a long moment of silence. Not the empty kind, but the full kind. The kind that feels like a door closing behind us, and another one creaking open.

For the first time in weeks, the air feels safe. And the house feels like it's holding us, instead of haunting us.

THIRTY FIVE

The bags are packed. The house is locked.

It feels surreal, like we've finally earned a pause. Like we're allowed to breathe without checking over our shoulders every few minutes.

Matt tosses our duffel bags into the backseat with a little more energy than I've seen in him lately. The morning air is cool, and he's wearing the same soft flannel hoodie I used to steal back when things were simple. Before everything happened.

Before her.

But today? Today feels different.

"Did you grab your charger?" I ask as he climbs into the driver's seat.

He holds it up like a trophy. "For once in my life, I came prepared."

I walk across the driveway. "Look at us. Functioning adults."

I stop next door. Hellen's already up, robe cinched tight, slippers on, a steaming mug of coffee in one hand and her other wrist deep in a bag of birdseed.

"Morning, sweetheart," she says when she sees me coming up the walk. "Off on your adventure?"

I nod. "Just for a few days. Everything's locked, but would you mind checking on the place while we're gone? Maybe grab the mail?"

She waves her hand. "Of course. You know I've got you. And if that weirdo comes back—" she lifts the bag of birdseed like a weapon—"she's gonna meet her match."

I laugh. "No violence, please. Just… call me. Okay?"

"Okay, but don't underestimate me," she says, then softens. "Be safe. And try to let yourself enjoy it."

I nod and head back to the car, where Matt's already queuing up a playlist like we're going cross-country.

He leans over as I climb in. "So... breakfast?"

We stop at The Brew Crew, our favorite time capsule. Same chalkboard menu, same sleepy barista with a half-formed man bun and a slow pour-over method that somehow makes the coffee taste better. But only when he makes it.

The moment we step inside, something in me exhales.

This place was ours before everything turned sideways. Before hospitals and journals and red notebooks and drawn-on smiley faces. Back when mornings meant something.

We order the same things we always did on dates: a vanilla cold brew for him, caramel latte for me, and one giant cinnamon roll to share because we always swear we won't finish it, and then always do.

We sit at our usual booth by the window. Sunlight filters through the glass in soft golden strips. The radio hums gently in the background. Today, it's not hard to hold a smile.

"I forgot what normal felt like," I say, picking a piece of the cinnamon roll apart.

Matt leans back in the booth, his arm stretched out along the backrest. "I didn't realize how much I missed it until we walked in here. It's like muscle memory."

I nod. "The good kind."

He grins. "You think it'll still be here in five years?"

"This place? Probably. That espresso machine will outlive all of us."

He laughs, and it hits me how good that sound feels. How much I missed it.

We finish the cinnamon roll and grab refills to go, then pile back into the car, lighter than when we started.

***

An hour out of town, we pull into a gas station to top off and grab snacks. It's the kind of place that smells like burnt hot dogs and sadness, but we don't care.

Matt grabs sour candy and trail mix. I go for pretzels and cherry gum. We're back to teasing each other over which snacks are superior and whether road trip playlists should include 90s hits or be legally required to feature at least one tragic acoustic cover.

It's normal. Playful. Free.

For a second, it feels like maybe we've done it, we've moved past her.

Matt goes to the bathroom again while I head back out to the car.

And everything shifts.

There's something tucked under the windshield wiper.

A single, folded square of paper, waiting like it's been there all along.

At first, I think it's a flyer. Or a coupon. Or some stupid gas station promotion.

But as I unfold it I see the handwriting. My stomach turns to ice.

Matt walks up behind me, whistling happily, eyes already narrowing. "What is that?"

I unfold the paper.

Leaving so soon? I had a full evening planned for us tonight.

Underneath is a street address. A time.

And at the very bottom… a hand-drawn smiley face.

Just like the one in the locker. Just like the first jar of Alfredo. Just like the twisted echo she's turned into a signature.

I drop the note like it might burn me.

"No. No, no, no—how?" I whisper, spinning around. I race back inside, nearly knocking over a display of windshield wipers and lottery tickets.

The cashier barely looks up. "Everything okay?"

"Do you have cameras? Facing the parking lot? Outside?" My voice is shaking.

He shakes his head. "Sorry. We haven't had working ones in like two years. Are you okay?!"

I bolt back outside and stop the nearest person getting gas, an older woman in a denim jacket pumping fuel into a minivan.

"Did you see anyone near my car?" I ask, pointing. "A girl, blonde, maybe standing right by the windshield?"

She frowns. "No. Just you two. Sorry."

I stand there, holding my breath. Matt walks over, the note clutched in his hand now.

We don't say anything at first.

We just look at each other.

Then the car.

"Do we call Harper?" I finally ask, my voice low. "Do we go home?"

Matt doesn't answer right away. He stares down at the paper. "Leaving so soon?"

"Do we cancel the trip? What if she's waiting there?!" I'm panting like a dog at this point.

He looks back up at me, his face unreadable.

"Or…" I swallow. "Do we go?"

His eyes flick to the note. Then back to me.

The weight of the question stretches between us like a tightrope.

Whatever we choose next, there won't be any more music and snacks.

THIRTY SIX

The silence in the car doesn't last long. It never does when panic meets principle.

Matt grips the steering wheel like it's the only thing keeping him grounded. We're not even halfway back to town when he finally says, "We need to call the police."

"No, we don't."

He glances at me, sharp. "Alice, she left a note. With a *time* and an *address*. That's not a prank. That's not just messing with us anymore. That's a direct threat."

"Exactly," I snap. "And where have the police been this whole time? Huh? Sitting around with their coffee and donuts, promising extra patrols and running in circles while she gets past everyone like she's made of smoke?"

Matt's jaw tightens. "Harper's doing what he can."

"No. Harper's doing what the system lets him do. And it hasn't worked."

His voice rises. "So what? We go *alone*? Just show up at some mystery address and hope for the best?"

I turn toward the window, heart pounding. "She wants *us* to show up. Not them. If we bring them into this, she'll vanish again. You know she will."

Matt exhales hard, knuckles white on the wheel. "You're acting like this is some story where you get to be the hero."

"I'm acting like someone who's *done* playing defense," I shoot back.

There's a long stretch of silence after that. Neither of us wins. Not really.

We pull into the driveway, gravel crunching under the tires. Hellen is on her porch like she's been waiting, wrapped in her cardigan, rocking slowly in that old chair that creaks like it's part of her bones.

She looks up and squints. "Back so soon? Forget something?"

I get out, suddenly exhausted. "Not exactly."

She gives me a look. "Uh-oh."

Matt doesn't come out right away. He's still in the car, staring at the note in his lap like it might rewrite itself if he glares long enough.

I walk over to Hellen and lean against the railing. "We didn't make it far."

"That part I noticed," she says, sipping from a chipped mug. "What happened?"

"She left another note," I say. "On my windshield. At the gas station. We were barely gone an hour. How did she even find us?"

Hellen's eyes darken. "Jesus."

"She gave an address. A time. Wants us to show up. Tonight."

There's a long pause. Just the sound of a bird somewhere nearby, the faint slam of a car door as Matt finally climbs out.

I look at her. "What would you do? If it was you? He wants me to call it in."

She studies me for a moment, then sets her mug down. "If it was me? I wouldn't trust these cops to finish the job. They're not all bad. But they're not all good either. And she's already proven she knows how to manipulate. How to disappear. How to *survive*."

I nod slowly.

Hellen leans forward slightly, her voice lower now. "But I'd also be careful not to let her turn you into her. You go charging in on your own, and it stops being about justice. Starts being about revenge. And that's a dangerous road."

"I'm already on it," I whisper.

She pats my hand gently. "Then don't walk it blind."

Matt disappears inside without saying much. I hear the sound of drawers slamming. A bag hitting the floor. Frustration echoes through every footstep.

I stay on the front steps for hours. I can't face him right now. I can't eat. I just sit.

The sky is now bleeding into orange and purple, the last rays of sunlight catching the edge of the roof like fire. The porch light hasn't kicked on yet, and I don't move to turn it on.

I just sit there. Breathing.

Listening.

Counting the seconds between his footsteps, between the creaks in the floorboards, between the steady, rising weight of the choice ahead of me.

To call the cops.

To ignore it.

To go.

One decision. Three lives. No way back.

The sun slips lower.

And I still don't know what I'm going to do.

THIRTY SEVEN

I don't know how I convinced Matt to do this.

Maybe it was the exhaustion. Maybe it was the way we both knew deep down that if we didn't show up, she'd vanish again. Slip through the cracks like smoke, just out of reach, and we'd be right back to the start. A different jar. A new message. Another ghost trail.

But mostly, I think it's because we're tired of running.

The police would only spook her. She'd bolt the second she saw sirens—or wouldn't show at all. And then what? Weeks of silence again? Another sleepless month of second-guessing every shadow, wondering what she's planning next?

No.

This ends now.

I keep telling myself she's not big enough to take us both down. Two against one. Logic over fear. And if I say it enough times in my head, maybe I'll believe it.

Matt doesn't say much on the drive. His hands grip the wheel hard, like they always do when he's trying not to feel anything. The silence between us hums like an electric current—tense, but solid. We're doing this together. Even if we're scared. Especially because we're scared.

We turn off the main road onto a long dirt drive that curves deep into a patch of woods. Trees lean overhead like they're trying to pull us in and swallow us whole. Weeds brush the sides of the truck, tall and dry like they haven't been disturbed in decades.

The deeper we go, the colder it feels.

I want to scream at Matt to turn around. Slam the gas, get us as far from here as possible. But I'm frozen in it. Stuck in the gravity of this place. Of what we're about to face.

Then we see it.

The trees part just enough to reveal it—a crumbling, two-story Victorian house crouched at the end of the path like a wounded animal waiting to bite.

I've lived here my entire life. I've never seen this place before.

How could something this massive be hiding right under our noses?

Matt cuts the engine. The headlights bathe the house in yellow light, making it look even more monstrous. A dying relic held together by rot and rusted nails.

The siding was once a soft blue, now stripped and sun-faded to a sickly gray. Broken shutters hang at crooked angles. Some are lying in pieces beneath shattered windows. The roof sags on one side like it's tired of holding itself up.

A tower rises on the left with a Victorian turret capped with an acorn-shaped roof that leans just slightly off center. Its windows are clouded with grime, curtains inside tattered and moving just slightly in the breeze like something breathed too close to them.

The porch is warped and brittle. Four or five cracked concrete steps lead to a small landing with a collapsed rocking chair and a broken flowerpot still filled with long-dead soil. Faded latticework wraps partway around the porch like it tried and failed to make the place look inviting once.

Vines snake up the railing and across the siding like veins, creeping up toward the second floor.

The door is barely hanging on. Slanted. Splintered. If I pushed it too hard, I'm not sure it would even resist.

Matt shifts in his seat, staring.

"Classic horror story house," I murmur.

He doesn't respond.

We sit in silence for a moment. Listening to the creak of trees in the wind. The occasional chirp of a bird that clearly hasn't learned better.

I glance down at the note still folded in my lap. The address. The time. The smiley face.

We're here.

I open the truck door. Gravel crunches beneath my boots. The smell of damp earth and mildew hits immediately, thick and wrong. I can feel the weight of the place pressing in on me like a warning.

Matt joins me on the passenger side.

We both stare at the steps.

"This is it," I say, though my voice barely makes it past my lips.

He nods once, jaw tight.

I turn to him. He's pale but steady. His eyes meet mine—tired, anxious, determined.

I reach out.

He takes my hand.

We stand like that for a second. Just breathing. Just holding on.

Then together, we step forward.

Toward the door. Toward the truth. Toward whatever waits for us inside.

THIRTY EIGHT

The door doesn't creak when we open it.

It groans.

Long and low like something wounded… and then it gives, slowly, like it's been waiting for us.

Matt steps in first, flashlight in hand, and I follow, one careful step at a time.

The smell hits immediately: old wood, mold, dust, and something sharp underneath it all. Chemical. Almost metallic. Like the residue of fear has seeped into the floorboards over time.

The beam of light cuts through the darkness, revealing warped walls and peeling wallpaper that once held color but now looks like bruised skin. The air is still. Heavy. As if the house is holding its breath.

We move forward, the floor beneath us groaning under every step.

Creak. Creak. Creak.

It's all I can hear now. That, and my heart in my ears.

There's no sign of her.

But I know she's here.

I *feel* it. The kind of silence that isn't empty—it's *watching*.

She's somewhere in this house. Sitting. Listening. Smiling.

We pass through what was once a living room. Torn curtains flutter from shattered windows. A couch skeleton leans to one side. There are blankets stacked in a corner, and an open book lying face-down on the floor next to a melted candle.

"She's been living here," I whisper.

Matt nods, jaw clenched. He shines the flashlight toward the fireplace. The ashes are cold and long dead, but there are footprints in the soot.

We move room to room. The air is getting thicker.

In the kitchen, everything stops.

Cans are lined neatly on the counters, corn, green beans, peaches, soup. They're all stacked like a storm bunker inventory. Next to them, boxes of matches, candles burned halfway down, plastic bottles filled with water.

And then I see them.

Jars.

About a dozen.

All Alfredo. All clean. All arranged in a perfect row on the back counter.

Each one marked with a smiley face.

Already prepared. Already waiting. As if we'd never left the game.

My stomach turns.

"She wasn't done," I whisper.

Matt doesn't speak. He just stares at the jars. Something dark settles behind his eyes, and I know he's thinking about his mother. About everything he never got to say.

I step closer to the window above the sink and freeze.

There's a car parked just behind the house. Hidden in the overgrowth.

Faded green. Beat-up. One headlight cracked.

I've seen it before.

At the grocery store. Parked behind the gas station.

Outside Hellen's house once, I thought it was one of her friends or family.

She's always been close.

Always watching.

We move toward the hallway at the back of the house, and that's when we see it.

The staircase.

It's worse than I expected. Warped. Crooked. Several steps splintered. One looks like it's already fallen through.

"This isn't safe," Matt says under his breath.

"No kidding."

We stare up into the shadowed second floor. The flashlight beam doesn't reach far enough to show anything but the railings, which sway slightly like they might collapse if you breathe too hard.

"Chris?" I call out.

Nothing.

"We don't feel comfortable climbing this," Matt adds. "Can you just… come down?"

Silence.

No creak. No voice. No movement.

Matt looks at me, and I already know what he's going to say.

"We shouldn't."

"She wants us to."

"She *wants* to watch us fall through this staircase and break our necks."

I don't argue. I just breathe. "If we don't go, we won't get answers."

He closes his eyes for a second. Then nods.

We climb.

One step at a time.

Each creak beneath our feet sounds like a scream. Each shift in the wood feels like it could be the last.

Halfway up, I look down and realize I'm shaking.

Matt reaches for my hand again. Holds it.

We keep moving.

Suddenly the flashbacks are hitting like hightide with every step. *Creak.* Chris laughing in my living room, one leg tucked beneath her, eating popcorn and complaining about the ending of a movie. *Creak.* Chris helping me alphabetize shelf labels at the store while

271

humming off-key. *Creak*. Chris bringing me soup when I had the flu and sitting by my bed like a sister.

I *loved* her.

Or at least, I loved who she let me see.

Now I'm climbing toward the part she never showed.

The part that's been waiting for this.

I know when I reach the top, I'll see her face. But it won't be her. Not *my* Chris.

Not anymore.

The landing is narrow. The floor slopes slightly to the left. Dust coats everything like a skin.

Matt points the flashlight down the hall.

At the far end, there's a soft glow, a flickering warmth behind a half-closed door.

We step forward, quiet, slow.

And then we hear it.

The soft *creak* of a rocking chair.

And the low, familiar hum of someone who's not humming for us.

Just for herself.

Just to pass the time.

THIRTY NINE

The creaking of the rocking chair slows.

The humming fades into a low, almost childlike murmur, like a lullaby she's been singing to herself for hours.

Matt and I freeze just outside the door.

The flickering candlelight leaks through the gap in the frame, casting jagged shadows across the hall. I can feel the warmth of it, unnatural against the cold stillness of the rest of the house.

I glance at Matt.

He nods, barely.

I reach out and push the door open.

Slowly.

The hinges squeal in protest, and what's inside unfolds one horrible inch at a time.

The room is glowing.

Candles cover every surface… lined on the windowsills, clustered on an old desk, set in bowls on the floor. Their light dances off the walls, and that's when I see them.

The smiley faces.

They cover everything.

Drawn in black ink, red pen, charcoal, eyeliner—any writing tool she could find.

Big ones. Tiny ones. Some grinning wide. Some smeared with thumbprints. Some so aggressively etched into the wall that the plaster is cracked around them.

Hundreds.

There's no pattern. No structure. Just repetition. Chaos. A war drum of mockery in ink.

I step inside, and the warmth of the candles wraps around me like a fever.

In the center of it all sits Chris.

In a wooden rocking chair that groans under her slow, steady rhythm.

She's barefoot.

Knees tucked up against her chest.

Hair long and tangled, draped over one shoulder like seaweed pulled from a lake.

There's a jar of Alfredo in her lap. She cradles it like it's glass-blown gold.

And she's smiling. Not the way she used to. This smile doesn't reach her eyes. Doesn't even try.

It's a performance.

A mask.

Behind it, I see everything she's lost, and everything she's decided to take back.

She stops rocking.

The room goes still.

Her gaze lifts and lands on me.

"Finally," she whispers, voice soft and sharp at the same time. "You made it."

Chris doesn't move.

She just watches us, bathed in candlelight, that calm smile fixed like it was stitched onto her face.

The room smells like wax and mildew and something faintly metallic. I take a step forward and notice the edge of a tattered teddy bear lying near the foot of the bed.

Next to it, a doll slumps sideways in a child-sized chair.

None of this makes sense, and yet it makes too much.

Matt stands stiff beside me. I can feel the heat rolling off him. Rage and grief and disbelief all pulsing under his skin.

Chris blinks slowly.

No one speaks.

She leans forward slightly in the rocking chair, still cradling the Alfredo jar like it's *precious*.

Then, from under her seat, she pulls out a folded piece of paper.

"I saved this for you," she says gently, reaching out with it.

Matt hesitates. I move first, take it from her fingers, and the moment I unfold it, the world tilts.

The handwriting.

I recognize it immediately.

It's the same soft loops and careful pressure from the journal.

Matt's mother's hand.

Don't trust anyone. Not even his father. Only you can know the truth. Find him. He will protect you.

- I love you, Mom.

The smiley face at the bottom is crooked. Wide. Drawn with a softer hand. Not Chris's.

Matt reads over my shoulder. His breath shallow.

Then he snaps. "Where's my mom?!"

The words echo off the walls.

For the first time, Chris's smile falters.

She closes her eyes. When she opens them again, they glisten.

"*Our* mom," she says softly. "She died. She died fighting for her life so that we could be free. Free and together."

Matt steps back, visibly shaking.

"You're lying," he whispers.

Chris tilts her head. "I'm not. She bought us time. She bought me a chance to find you."

There's no drama in her voice. No theatrics. Just… truth. Measured and calm.

"She told me stories about you, Matt. About how smart you were. How careful. How much she missed your laugh. And when I finally escaped, when I made it out—I made a promise. That I'd find you. That I'd give you the family you never got."

Matt is frozen. A statue carved from grief.

I force my voice to work. "And what? That included stalking us? Manipulating us? Gaslighting me into thinking I was losing my mind?"

Chris's head tilts again, like I'm the one not making sense.

"I had to know what kind of girl had my brother's heart," she says. "At first, I just wanted you gone. I didn't like how soft he got when you were around. How distracted. So I planted little things. Things I knew would make you fight. Would make you question him."

My throat tightens. "Like the mail? The coffee on top of my car? The notes in my locker."

She nods, enthusiastically. "But then something shifted. I realized you weren't just in the way. You were… well Alice, you were just better at it."

I blink. "At what?"

"The game, of course," she says, smiling again. "You caught on. Unlike *him*." She glances at Matt with a look of disappointment. "You pushed back. You didn't just fall apart, you fought. And suddenly, you weren't a problem. You were a... challenge."

Matt lets out a breath like he's choking on it. "You were *toying* with us."

"I was learning," Chris replies, calm as ever. "About the two of you. About where I fit in. About what makes you *tick*."

She looks down at the jar in her lap and runs her finger along the label.

"I just wanted my family. That's *all* this ever was supposed to be..."

A silence spreads between us, thick and unbearable.

I take a step forward, jaw tight. "If all of this was just to be with your brother again... then *why me?* Why bring me into it? Why torture me?"

Chris lifts her eyes to mine.

Her voice is steady. Soft.

"Because at first, I wanted to remove you. But then..." She smiles again. "I saw how much fun it could

279

be. You were so good at the game, Alice. You made me work for it. *You* made it matter." Another ugly look in Matts direction.

"Honestly Matthew, Mom painted you as such a hero. Such a protector. She went on and on about how strong you were. What kind of hero can't even push through his own emotions and *get it together*? You couldn't even open moms journal. That's no hero. It's a coward."

I stare at her.

At the candlelight reflected in her irises. At the madness dressed in calm.

And I realize that to her, this was *never* about hate.

It was about belonging.

And control.

FORTY

The room feels too still.

Candles flicker across the walls, casting soft, warping shadows across Chris's face. She sits in the old rocking chair like it's a throne, calm and radiant in her own twisted way. Her hands rest folded in her lap. Her feet don't even touch the floor.

The silence stretches, thick and oppressive, broken only by the slow creak-creak-creak of the chair.

Matt stands beside me, tense. I can feel the heat rolling off him. His fists are clenched, his jaw tight. I want to reach for his hand, but I don't. Not yet. Not here.

Chris tilts her head slightly and smiles like we're old friends catching up over tea.

"I always wondered what it would feel like," she says softly. "To be the one in control."

No one responds. She lets her words linger like perfume in the air, then continues.

"For so long, I was a prisoner. Not just physically—but mentally. Every move was decided for me. When to eat. When to sleep. When I was allowed to speak." Her eyes don't blink. "My mother used to tell me stories. She would whisper them to me at night when he couldn't hear. She said, 'One day, you'll be free. And when you are, you won't just survive. You'll *create*.'"

Chris rocks gently in the chair, humming now. The smile never leaves her face.

It's the humming that starts to twist my stomach into knots.

Just a low, syrupy tune—off-key in a way that doesn't feel accidental. Her eyes are half-lidded, and she's not looking at us anymore. She's somewhere else entirely.

"She used to say it when things got really bad," she whispers after a beat. "When I couldn't stop crying, when there was blood on the floor, when he locked her in the basement. She would look at me with her bruised face and say, 'You just have to keep a smile on.'"

The creaking of the rocking chair fills the silence like a metronome counting down to something awful.

Chris starts to sing.

"Keep a smile on, little one, even when the lights go out.
Keep a smile on, baby girl, don't you scream, don't you shout…"

Her voice is soft and eerily childlike. I glance at Matt, who looks just as shaken as I feel. I hear him mumble very quietly under his breath. "That's not the words." Low enough she doesn't hear.

His eyes are locked on her, like he's trying to figure out what version of his sister is in front of him right now.

"Chris?" I ask carefully. "Christina?"

She stops rocking.

The air goes cold.

Then her voice—no longer soft, no longer childlike—slices through the space between us.

"**DON'T** call me Christina."

I flinch.

"My name is Chris," she says firmly, slowly standing to her feet. "*He* called me Christina. *He*

283

whispered it like a curse. My mother only said it when she was afraid. When she needed me to *hide*."

Matt shifts beside me. Chris notices.

"She believed in me," she says. "She believed I was meant for something *greater* than rotting away down there like *she* did."

"You think this is greater?" Matt snaps. "Stalking people? Hurting them? Manipulating everyone around you like we're pawns in your little psychotic board game?"

Her smile doesn't falter. "I gave your life purpose, Matthew. I brought you closer to the truth than anyone else ever dared."

Matt takes a step forward. "You *kidnapped me.* You drugged me. You left a trail of lies and destruction—"

"I led you to answers," Chris says, still perfectly calm. "All the years you spent begging for someone to believe you... and here I am. The missing piece. The story your father tried to bury."

"You're not a piece of anything," he growls. "You're a virus. Infecting everything and everyone."

Her smile falters.

Her eyes darken—not with rage, but with something colder. Older. Haunted.

"You sound just like him," she says, sounding wounded, voice barely above a whisper.

Matt freezes.

Chris steps forward, slowly, like a puppet on invisible strings. Her shadow stretches across the floor toward us like a stain.

"You think raising your voice gives you control?" she says. "That men can just bark and take what they want?"

"No, I—"

Her voice cracks. "*He* said the same things. 'You're broken.' 'You're poison.' 'You ruin everything you touch.' He said all of that, too—right before he locked my mother in a room and beat her so badly she couldn't walk for three days."

The temperature in the room drops ten degrees. I can barely breathe.

"You think I didn't know?! That I wasn't old enough to understand what was happening?!" She smashes the jar of sauce on the floor in the corner of the room. "I *saw* what he did! I *heard* the things he said!"

I flinch and Matt steps between us. "Chris, you don't have to do this—"

"Don't **YOU** start," she spits. "You don't get to play protector now. You weren't there! You were out living your happy little life while I was counting ceiling tiles and wondering if today was the day she'd finally disappear for good."

"I'm not him, Chris," Matt says, but his voice is softer now. "I swear to God, I'm not him. I didn't know you existed."

"**BUT YOU SOUND JUST LIKE HIM!**" She screams. "They erased me! Just like they erased *her*! Buried us both so deep no one even remembered we were real!"

Matt steps forward again, trying to stay calm. "You are real. You're right here. But this—this isn't how you reconnect with someone. You kidnapped me. You stalked Alice. You left blood and chaos like it was proof of something."

"You think you're the only one who *bleeds*?" she hisses. "You think you can walk in here, raise your voice like he did, and suddenly you're the one in charge? No.

I'm the one in control now. Me. *That's* what this is about."

Her eyes flicker with something dark and breaking. "This is the first time in my *entire life* that I've had all the pieces. That *I've* been in charge of the story. And I'm not letting it go."

"Then tell the story, Chris," he says. "Tell it. Let us help you."

Her breath quickens.

"I. DON'T. NEED. HELP!" she explodes.

And then it shatters.

Chris moves faster than I've ever seen her. She snatches something off the table behind her—a jagged shard of glass from the broken window next to her.

She lunges.

Matt shouts and raises his arms. The glass catches the edge of his shoulder, slicing deep. Blood spills instantly, dark and vivid across his shirt.

"Chris—STOP!" I cry out.

She's not listening.

"You're not safe like she said!" she screams. "You're just like *HIM*!"

Matt stumbles backward, crashing into the wall with a grunt. Blood drips down his forearm, staining the wood floor in thick, sticky splatters.

My ears ring.

I move before I can think—just a few steps toward him, trying to get between them—but I see the blood again, too much of it, too bright. My vision tunnels. The air turns thick and wrong.

I reach for Matt's arm.

Then everything tilts.

The sound of my name, Matt yelling it—

The sound of Chris wailing, *"You're just like him!"*

And then nothing.

Just blackness, swallowing me whole.

FORTY ONE

There's nothing.

No sound. No light. No air.

Just the suffocating weight of blackness.

My eyes open—at least, I think they do—but it makes no difference. I can't see anything. Not my hands. Not the floor beneath me. Just the kind of pitch-dark that feels alive, like it's pressing against my skin.

I try to sit up.

Pain screams down the side of my neck, into my shoulder, into the base of my spine. The floor is cold, concrete maybe, and every muscle in my body feels like it's been wrung out.

What happened?

The question crashes into me with a wave of nausea. Images flicker through my mind like broken film—Chris's voice, glass flashing, Matt's blood, and then…

Oh God.

"Matt." I whisper it, but there's no echo. The silence is too dense. My throat is raw, dry, like sandpaper scraped down my windpipe.

I shift onto my hands and knees, heart hammering. The floor is slick in spots—maybe condensation, maybe something worse—but I keep crawling. There has to be a wall. A door. A switch.

My hands graze something cool and metallic. A smooth edge. A wall-mounted box?

I feel for a corner. Then a switch.

Click.

A dim overhead bulb sputters, flickers, then floods the space with a weak yellow glow. It's the same kind of bulb that hangs in Matt's garage. It buzzes softly, casting harsh shadows across rough concrete walls.

And suddenly, I see everything.

It's a room. Maybe ten feet by ten feet, bare and windowless. The ceiling's low. The walls are made entirely of unpainted cement. And tucked into one corner is a built-in desk—more like a shelf hammered into the wall—with a metal folding chair beside it.

On the desk sits a chipped plate with cold ravioli, stiff and congealed, and three bottles of water lined up like offerings.

I crawl to the desk, my eyes barely able to withstand the pressure.

"Did you put the entire sun inside one light bulb?!" *Fuck, my head hurts.*

I reach for a bottle, twist the cap.

And stop.

My fingers freeze around the plastic. Every instinct screams *don't trust it.* What if it's drugged? What if Chris poisoned it? This is exactly the kind of mind game she'd play.

But the fire in my throat is worse than fear. Trembling, I lift it to my lips and sip. It's clean. *I think.* Room temperature. I swallow again, greedily now, the ache in my throat easing with each gulp.

When I lower the bottle, I feel lightheaded. Not from the water—but from the reality pressing in on me.

I stumble to my feet and turn in a slow circle.

To the left of the desk, stacked neatly along the floor, is a pile of notebooks—some pristine, some frayed. I pick one up. The handwriting is delicate, looping. Familiar.

It's hers. Matt's mother.

"Today, we practiced multiplication. She's learning fast. She asks about the sun sometimes. I lie and tell her it's cloudy again."

Another page:

"She cried for two hours when the door slammed. I didn't have the words to comfort her. I just held her and told her the same thing I always do, you just have to keep a smile on."

I pull out another notebook. The handwriting is messier—childish, uncertain. Letters written backwards. A little girl trying to learn.

"Red is my favorite color. Mommy said it means strong. I want to be red someday."

"Today I spelled all the days of the week without messing up! Mom gave me some chocolate."

Bile rises in my throat. I drop the notebook and back away, but my heel hits something soft. I whirl.

A pile of pillows and blankets. Nestled in the far corner like a makeshift bed. Threadbare. Faded. One of the blankets has a smiley face stitched into the corner in uneven red thread.

I can't do this.

I'm in the place Chris was raised. Trapped. Like her mother.

I turn to the opposite wall. There's a door—metal, bolted, rust staining the edges. I press my hand against it, then both hands, then throw my weight against it.

It doesn't budge.

There's a latch on the outside. And I'm locked in.

I step back, chest heaving. My lungs won't fill. The air is heavy with history and ghosts. My gaze sweeps the room one last time—and then I see it.

A jacket.

Matt's.

Crumpled in the corner beneath the desk. I drop to my knees and grab it, my hands clutching the soft, familiar fabric like a lifeline.

He was here.

He was here. Just like I am now.

Something inside me breaks.

A sharp, splintering sound deep in my chest. I curl up on the cold floor, still holding the jacket to my face. The scent of him clings faintly to the collar. I close my eyes and let the sobs take me. I don't care how loud I am. I don't care if she hears.

Let her.

I cry until my ribs ache. Until my fingers go numb.

And then—just as I start to drift into that numb space, a low hum vibrates through the ceiling.

A mechanical sound. A click.

My head jerks up.

There, in the corner, nearly hidden in shadow, a speaker embedded in the wall buzzes to life.

A voice follows.

Sweet. Calm. Perfectly composed.

"Good. You're awake. Please eat."

FORTY TWO

The speaker clicks again with a soft buzz.

That sound alone is enough to set me off.

I shoot to my feet, still gripping Matt's jacket, and launch it at the nearest wall. The bottle of water on the desk crashes down next, skidding across the concrete.

"Where is he?!" I scream, my voice echoing wildly off the walls. "Chris! What the hell did you do to him?"

Silence.

"Let me out! Right now! This isn't a game anymore—do you hear me? Let me out!"

I grab the plate of ravioli and hurl it at the speaker. It hits the ceiling near the corner and drops with a clatter. My chest is heaving, fists clenched so tight my nails dig into my palms.

Then—like a goddamn horror movie—the speaker crackles back to life.

"I'm sorry," Chris says sweetly. "Are you feeling a little dramatic this morning?"

"Don't start with me. Tell me where Matt is!"

"Matt's fine. He always is. He's very resilient. He always finds someone to save him, don't you think?"

I shake my head. "You're insane."

"And yet you trusted me for months," she hums.

"You manipulated me. You pretended to be my friend while stalking my life!"

"I didn't pretend," Chris replies, soft now. "I *was* your friend, Alice. I still am. We had so many good times together, didn't we?"

My mouth opens to argue—but then stalls.

Because the worst part is… we did.

I feel a sharp ache in my chest as my knees wobble, and I slowly sink down onto the floor.

"Remember Brew Crew mornings?" Chris says, like she's reading my mind. "You'd always try to sneak in the back door without the bell chiming, like that would spare you the customer service smiles. And I'd bring you a cookie even when you told me not to. But then you'd eat it anyway."

I say nothing. My throat's tight.

Chris keeps going.

"That Halloween shift where you dressed up as a tired grocery employee—which was just you in your regular uniform, but with a plastic spider taped to your shoulder. I told you that was lazy. You told me to shut up and gave me a pumpkin donut."

I close my eyes.

"We laughed a lot," she adds quietly. "You made me feel normal."

My voice cracks. "We weren't friends. I didn't know who you were."

"You knew *exactly* who I was," she says, more firmly now. "I'm the only one who ever saw you. I listened. I remembered everything. The coffee orders. Your weird book rants. How you get those little anxiety twitches in your left hand when you're about to cry."

The speaker hums again, and I swear I hear her sit down wherever she is—like this is just another late-night phone call between friends.

"You really don't get it yet, do you?" she says. "All this time, I wasn't trying to be close to Matt. I was trying to be close to you. You made me want more. You reminded me of the girl my mother described in all those bedtime stories. The one with freedom and fire and so much loneliness she didn't even know it was there."

I blink. My eyes drift across the room—to the desk, to the books, to the walls, and then back to Matt's jacket in the corner.

Reality crashes in all over again.

He was here. And I am not free.

My rage returns, sudden and searing.

I stand up again, fists clenched at my sides.

"Chris," I say, steady but shaking, "you have to let me out of here."

Silence.

Then, the soft hum of the speaker again.

"Alice," she says gently, almost lovingly.

"You're already out."

A pause.

Then her voice, light and childlike:

"You're me now. And I'm you. The girl with all the fire and all the freedom."

FORTY THREE

I don't know what day it is anymore.

The lights go off at the same time every night and flicker back on with the same dull hum each morning. Chris brings me food—sometimes warm, sometimes not. Always just enough to keep me alive.

Water bottles, rationed.

Books to read. Sometimes even a crossword puzzle.

She talks through the speaker. Never in person.

At first, I screamed every time it clicked on. I begged. Pleaded. Bargained.

Then I stopped.

Now I answer softly. I ask questions. I mimic her tone. I wait.

Because Chris isn't just trying to control me. She's trying to remake me.

And I've started letting her believe it's working.

Today, the lights blink on slower than usual. It takes me a second to adjust. The bulb overhead hums weakly. My throat's dry, but the water ration sits untouched. I'm learning not to drink too fast or too much.

The speaker clicks on.

"Good morning, Christina!"

Her voice is too sweet.

"Good morning, Alice." I answer quietly, still curled in my blanket on the floor.

"I have a surprise for you."

That sentence alone makes my stomach twist.

A few minutes later, a drawer in the wall clicks open, like it's being unlocked from somewhere else. Inside is a granola bar and a folded t-shirt.

The shirt is plain. Black. My size. But across the chest in white letters is a single word:

CHRIS.

I stare at it for too long. The speaker clicks again.

"It's time," she says. "The name Alice is no longer yours. It's mine."

My mouth is dry. "What if I say no?"

A pause.

"Then you don't eat."

I grip the edge of the drawer.

The air feels thinner.

"You want me to be you," I say slowly, "but I don't know how."

"Learn," she answers.

"Then teach me."

A beat of silence.

Then she laughs—a breathy, delighted sound. Like I've just played the game right.

"You're learning," she says. "Good girl."

I press on, carefully. "If you want me to *really* be you… I need to understand. Not just the clothes or the name. I need to know *why*. Why the smiley face? Why the games? Why me?"

The speaker hums.

"You know," she says finally, "you always were the *smartest* friend I had."

Another click. A pause.

Then a longer buzz—and her voice is softer.

"My mom used to draw them," she says.

"Everywhere. On the walls. On scraps of paper. She'd dip her finger in old food or dirt or ash and just draw them on the concrete. It was… something to look at that wasn't him."

I say nothing. Just let her speak.

"When things got bad, she'd hold my hand and whisper, 'Keep a smile on, baby. If he sees fear, he wins.'" Chris laughs under her breath. "That's why I carved it into everything. Drew it. Tattooed it onto this life like armor. It's the only way I ever felt protected."

Her voice trembles for the first time. Just slightly.

"One night, he came home angry. I don't remember why. Maybe the stove didn't light right. Maybe he thought my mom blinked at him the wrong way. Doesn't matter. He pulled her by the hair, dragged her across the room. I hid behind the shelves, holding one of the smiley face pages she gave me. I squeezed it so tight my fingernails ripped it in half."

My stomach turns.

"Afterward, she couldn't stand. He locked her behind the heavy door for three days. I thought she was dead." Chris pauses. "I laid outside that door and hummed the smiley face song until I passed out."

I wrap Matt's jacket tighter around my body. "That's… horrible."

"That's life," she says flatly. "But now you understand."

I close my eyes.

"You didn't deserve that," I whisper.

Now it's my turn.

"My mom used to let me play in the rain," I say quietly. "Said I could make friends with the worms if I was lonely. For a long time, I didn't have anyone but them."

A pause. I wait to see if she'll laugh. She doesn't.

"Then I met Bridgette. She was everything I wasn't—loud, fearless, magnetic. Her twin sister, Cassie, was quiet, never really liked me. But Bridgette? She saved me."

I feel tears press at the edges of my eyes, but I keep going.

"We did everything together. Shared everything with each other. From little crushes to heartbreaks. First dreams. For a while, I thought maybe… maybe life wouldn't be so lonely."

I press my forehead to my knees.

"But one day they didn't show up at the bus stop. They weren't at lunch. When I got home, my mom was crying on the phone. Their dad had a breakdown. Killed both girls. Killed their mother. He never even told anyone where the bodies were. Just confessed and clammed up."

Chris says nothing.

"I kept trying to run away. Thought maybe I could find them. I was nine. They sent me to therapy. I never spoke much. But sometimes I wonder if I died back then, too. If I ever really came back."

The speaker is silent.

Then finally—

"…That's why you're strong."

I shake my head. "No. That's why I don't trust anything good. Why I never feel safe."

Chris exhales like she understands.

"You're getting it now," she says.

"What?"

"This is what makes us the same. The broken girls. The forgotten girls. The ones no one came back for."

She lets the words sink in, and I can feel her watching again—through a camera, a vent, some dark unseen corner.

"Say it," she murmurs.

I lift my chin. Swallow.

"…Okay. I'm Chris."

"Good girl," she says. I can hear her smirk like we were back joking together on the bread aisle at work.

But I don't feel good. I feel like the walls just got smaller.

FORTY FOUR

The lights never go fully dark down here.

Even when they dim for "sleep hours"—which I've stopped trying to track—they hum faintly above me, buzzing like a fly that won't die. It's enough to keep your brain in a half-state; never fully rested, never fully awake. Just suspended. Like meat in a freezer.

I lay flat on the thin cot bolted to the floor. The mattress is too firm, too flat. My back aches, and I don't know how long I've been down here. Time drips like water, torture. No clocks. No sun. Just the steady *drip… drip… drip* from a rusted pipe and the sound of my own blood in my ears.

Matt's jacket is folded neatly next to me, just like she left it. A trophy. A warning. A game piece. I've stopped touching it. I've stopped crying into it. It smells less like him and more like dust now.

I sit up slowly, spine stiff and burning. I breathe through it. I have to.

She's watching. I know she is. Maybe not every second, but often enough that I can't let my guard drop.

And the speaker? It's alive. It crackles sometimes, even when she's not speaking. I hate it. I *hate* all of it.

I look up at it now, and I smile. "Thank you for the food today."

It wasn't food. It was powdered soup and a dry granola bar. But I say it sweetly anyway.

The speaker clicks. Not a word, just… a click. A little reminder. *I'm here. I'm listening.*

Good. Listen, you psycho.

Inside, I am *screaming.*

You think I'm your little project? That you can cut me off from the world and mold me into something that fits the twisted fantasy playing on repeat in your head?

You're wrong. You don't know me.

I press my palms together in my lap to keep them from shaking. Not from fear—no, that passed days ago. This is rage. Cold, patient, caged rage.

She wants me to crack. She wants me to beg. To scream. To become her.

But I won't.

I smile. I nod. I speak softly. I keep my tone measured. I look like the version of me she wants me to be.

And I plan.

I study every inch of this place every time I'm awake. I count steps from the cot to the sink. I listen to the sounds that echo behind the walls. I've started mapping them out in my head.

You left me alive, Chris. *You shouldn't have.*

One day, I'll see you again. Not on a fuzzy screen or through a crackling speaker. No, you'll stand in front of me, and when you do, I'll show you exactly what you made.

And I promise you—whatever you've done to Matt, wherever you've put Christina—I will make you answer for every second of it.

Until then, I smile. I eat the poison food. I sleep beneath the humming lights. I wear the skin she expects me to wear.

But the *real* me?

She's sharpening her teeth in the dark.

I tilt my head, just like I know she wants me to.

And then I hear it.

A thump.

A metal scrape.

The drawer. The one across the room that I've avoided opening.

The speaker clicks again—this time louder, firmer.

"You're ready now," her voice filters through, bright and sugary. "Look in the drawer, Alice."

My mouth dries. Every instinct in me screams to stay put. But I rise, barefoot against the cold cement. I walk slowly toward the drawer, heart pounding like it's trying to punch its way out of my chest.

I reach down.

Pull the handle.

Inside is a neatly folded outfit: a pale yellow sundress, a brown cardigan, and a pair of familiar Vans.

My breath catches in my throat. The same outfit she wore the day she visited me in the hospital.

"You see?" her voice sings from the speaker. "You're starting to understand. We're not so different."

I back away from the drawer like it bit me. My knees hit the cot, and I sit hard.

I want to scream. I want to tear the clothes apart, spit in the camera, and curse her name. I want to shout *I am not you!* until my voice rips in two.

But I don't.

Because she's watching.

Because I don't know what happens if I say no.

I sit there, staring at the pile of clothes like it's a venomous snake.

"Put them on," she coos through the speaker. "It's time."

Silence follows.

Then the crackle fades.

I stare at the outfit. My skin itches. My stomach rolls. I feel like I'm being stitched into a skin that isn't mine. But I reach out.

I lift the cardigan with shaking hands.

This doesn't mean I believe her.

This doesn't mean she's winning.

This means *I'm surviving.*

I put on the dress. Slowly. One piece at a time. The fabric feels too soft, too personal. A costume. A cage.

I sit back down, legs crossed, eyes locked on the red light of the camera.

You want me to play your game, Chris?

Fine.

I'll play it.

But you better pray I don't win.

FORTY FIVE

It's been two days.

Two long, silent, maddening days.

No clocks. No windows. Just the steady hum of ventilation and the subtle vibration of power behind the walls. The lights never dim, never flicker — always sterile, always watching. If there's a camera in here, I haven't found it. But I know it's there. Chris is always watching.

I've barely slept. Barely eaten. The food that appears at the door is bland, texture less, and always portioned the same. I eat it anyway. I don't want to give her the satisfaction of watching me fall apart.

The clothes — the goddamn clothes — sit folded neatly on the edge of the cot. *Mocking* me. A yellow sundress, almost identical to the one she wore at the hospital. White lace trim, soft fabric, tailored like it was made *for me*. There's even a pair of those same worn-in Vans she always wore. Her uniform. Or rather… mine now?

I asked about Matt. I screamed his name into the empty vents. I cried and begged and tore the blanket into strips. Chris never answered.

But later that day, a note was slipped under the door.

Three words, in tidy handwriting.

Christina wouldn't cry..

I wanted to rip the paper to shreds. Instead, I folded it and tucked it into the waistband of my pants. Just in case.

Now, sitting here, I stare at the clothes again. I haven't touched them since that night. But I know this silence won't last much longer. She's letting me marinate in my own dread — that's part of the game. I don't know what happens when I put them on… but I do know what happens if I don't.

I stand. My knees pop, my body aching from too much stillness. I peel off the sweatshirt and jeans I've been clinging to like armor and pick up the sundress. The fabric is soft in my fingers, like it's been washed a

313

hundred times. Like hers always looked. The shoes fit too perfectly. I hate that.

I catch my reflection in the metal panel above the sink. My hair's a mess, my eyes hollow. But in this dress, with my arms bare and the shoes tight on my feet, I do look like her. And that makes my stomach turn.

A voice crackles through the speaker, distorted but unmistakable.

"You look beautiful."

I clench my jaw and force myself to breathe. I will not break. Not yet.

"Is this what you wanted?" I say to the ceiling.

There's a pause. Then, with a strange warmth that makes my skin crawl: *"Now we can begin."*

***

The next morning, the voice wakes me.

"Rise and shine, Christina."

It crackles through the ceiling like a morning prayer— sickeningly cheerful. I sit up on the cot, stomach twisting, dress clinging to me like it's part of my skin now. I haven't taken it off. She hasn't told me to.

"I have a surprise for you today," she continues, chipper and bright, like some twisted talk show host. "Let's see how much you've *remembered*."

I don't respond. I haven't responded to anything she's said since I put on the dress. If she wants a performance, she can earn it.

The speaker goes silent.

A soft mechanical *click* comes from the far wall. The door — the one that's been sealed since I arrived — slowly slides open. Light pours in from a hallway I didn't know existed. Pale blue walls. Carpet. It looks like a suburban office building.

This has to be a trick.

I step through cautiously, my feet cold in the worn Vans. The air smells... clean. Not like bleach-clean, but air-freshener clean. Lavender. Comforting. Manufactured.

At the end of the hallway is another room — brighter, filled with daylight lamps and retro furniture. It looks like a living room from a sitcom. Mismatched throw pillows, a worn coffee table, and a couch facing

315

an old box TV. Everything is faded and cheerful in that *too perfect* way.

There's a board game on the coffee table. Candyland. Figures.

Next to it, a card. Handwritten.

"Let's make today fun. If you win, I'll answer a question. One. Your choice."

I grip the edge of the table so hard my knuckles go white. I should kick it over. I should scream into the air vents until my throat bleeds.

But instead, I sit.

Because she knows I'll play.

I start flipping cards, moving the little gingerbread man across the board. It's mindless. Humiliating. But with every space, I'm closer to that single question.

When I finally win — if you can even call it that — her voice returns.

"Well done, Christina. See? You remember how to have fun after all."

My throat is dry. I close my eyes and force the words out.

"What did you do with Matt?"

A pause.

Then: *Static.*

That's all.

I wait, breath caught in my chest. The TV clicks on by itself. Old cartoons. Looney Tunes, I think.

Her voice again, faintly.

"Wrong question."

I scream. I flip the board. I throw one of the pillows across the room so hard it hits the TV screen.

The speaker clicks off.

She doesn't come back.

Not for hours.

And when she does, all she says is: "Try again tomorrow."

A soft *clunk* drops from the chute behind me.

I turn slowly.

No food tray. No water bottle. Just a small black case, resting perfectly upright like someone placed it there by hand.

I don't want to open it. But I already know I will.

Inside: A syringe, capped.

A tiny vial of clear liquid.

And a note folded in half with deliberate neatness.

"Trust fall, Christina. Sweet dreams."

Smiley face, drawn in thick black ink.

The speaker clicks on.

"You've earned a break," Chris says, her voice too sweet. "But only if you're brave."

My stomach knots. "What is it?"

"A lullaby," she answers simply. "We can't have you peeking during setup, now can we?"

Silence stretches.

"Of course," she adds, "I could come down and do it for you. Strap you down like he used to. But that's not the game, is it? If you're really me, you'd never let someone else hold the needle."

I clench my jaw.

This is control wrapped in ribbons. Another sick performance. She wants me to participate—to make me responsible for my own sedation. So I can wake up wondering what I missed, what she touched, what she left.

I almost hurl the case across the room. I almost scream into the camera, tear the speaker from the wall, anything—

But my hand is already picking up the vial.

"Good girl," she coos.

I draw the liquid into the syringe with trembling fingers. It's clear. Odorless. Nothing.

I sit on the edge of the cot, press the needle to the soft flesh of my thigh, and close my eyes.

"You're getting better at letting go," she whispers.

I push the plunger down.

Everything tilts sideways.

And then the dark swallows me whole.

FORTY SIX

The light clicks on with a soft hum, snapping me awake.

I don't remember falling asleep. Time bleeds together down here—mornings don't mean anything. There's no sun, just the same flickering overhead bulb that decides when I've earned light again.

Something's different today.

The desk that's usually bare now holds three things:

A handheld mirror.

A black dry-erase marker.

And a small yellow note with a smiley face drawn on it—two dots, curved mouth, no words.

I already feel the dread blooming in my throat, but I cross the room anyway. There's no sound—just the faint buzz of electricity and my bare feet scuffing across concrete. I pick up the mirror. It's round, child-sized, like something from a makeup kit. My reflection stares back: pale, gaunt, cracked lips, eyes that don't blink fast enough to be alive.

The speaker clicks on.

"Good morning, sunshine."

Chris's voice is bright, sugar-laced and brittle. I don't answer. I've learned it doesn't help.

"I thought we'd play a little game today. You've been looking so sad lately, and it's honestly bringing the whole mood down. So let's fix that."

I glance back at the mirror. The note. The marker.

"It's easy," she coos. "You're going to draw a smile. Right across that lovely mouth of yours. And then you're going to hold it for ten minutes."

A beat. Then she adds, chipper, "No blinking. No frowning. No crying. Just… smile."

A beep sounds. A red digital timer above the door clicks on: **00:00:00**.

I almost laugh. It's absurd. But I don't laugh. Because I know what happens when I don't play along.

My hands shake as I uncap the marker.

I drag the tip across my cheeks, curving the black line up at each end like a clown mask. My reflection becomes grotesque. The smiley face doesn't match my eyes. They're hollow, bloodshot, wrong.

The timer beeps again—**00:10:00** appears—and begins to count down.

"Good girl," Chris whispers through the speaker.

I stare into my reflection and try to hold it.

One second. Two. Five.

The black line starts to itch against my skin. My face feels like it's cracking in half.

"You know," Chris says conversationally, "my mom used to make me smile when I wanted to cry. She'd say, *You just have to keep a smile on, honey. That's how we survive.'* Sweet, right?"

No. But I don't move.

She keeps talking.

"She smiled even when she bled. Even when he came down the stairs. You could see it in her teeth— like she was trying to pretend we were somewhere else. And I believed her. I did. For years, I thought maybe we were."

My lips twitch. I almost break.

The buzzer blares—deafening, disorienting. The lights flash red.

The timer resets: **00:10:00.**

"You frowned," Chris says flatly. "Start over."

I bite the inside of my cheek so hard I taste blood.

This time, I don't draw a new smile. I just force my mouth into one. It feels foreign, unnatural, painful.

"I used to think she smiled for me," Chris murmurs. "But she didn't. She smiled for herself. Because that's all we ever have, isn't it? Ourselves. Everyone else just... disappoints."

The timer ticks. **00:09:12.**

I keep smiling. My cheeks ache. My jaw trembles.

Chris hums a tune—soft and sweet. It takes me a minute to recognize it.

If you're happy and you know it...

I close my eyes.

"Open them," she snaps. "Eyes on the prize, Alice."

I open them. The mirror's still there.

Only now, something's playing behind my reflection.

It's a recording. Static-laced. A woman—young, bruised, trembling—smiling into a camera. Her eyes shine with tears, but her lips stay stretched wide.

"My name is—"

The tape skips.

"You just have to keep a smile on."

Skip.

"We're fine. We're fine. We're fine."

Then silence.

I realize with a jolt: it's Chris's mother.

The timer ticks down. **00:03:48.**

Chris says nothing. The speaker hums quietly, like she's savoring the moment.

I want to scream. I want to punch the mirror, claw the marker off my face, tear down the camera I know is watching. But I don't. I keep smiling. Because that's what she wants.

And maybe, just maybe, I want to see how far she'll take it.

00:00:04.

00:00:03.

00:00:02.

00:00:01.

The buzzer doesn't go off. The lights stay on. Then the speaker clicks again.

"…See? It's not so hard. You're getting better. I almost believed you liked it."

The timer vanishes. The door stays locked.

But in the corner of the desk, something new appears: A cupcake with a single, crooked candle.

And a note: *Tomorrow, we celebrate.*

I move to the cot slowly, eyes stinging, heart slamming against my ribs. My body's stiff. Numb. My smile smeared and ghosted across my skin.

And then I hear it.

Clunk.

The chute opens. Another black case.

I don't need to ask what it is.

The same syringe. The same clear vial. The same note.

Rest well, Christina. You'll need your strength.

Signed with a smiley face.

The speaker hisses back to life.

"Take your medicine."

"Already?"

I almost don't. I want to rebel, to scream something back, to throw the syringe into the wall.

But if I don't… the next game will be worse. She'll make sure of it.

My hand shakes as I draw the liquid.

My skin burns as the needle breaks through.

The last thing I hear is her voice, soft and low:

"Goodnight, me."

FORTY SEVEN

I wake to the sound of music.

Tinny, off-key notes echo through the room—
Happy Birthday to You, slowed down just enough to
sound wrong. A warped music box melody. I sit up on
the cot, heart pounding, and stare.

The room has changed.

Balloons hang from the ceiling, half-deflated and
mismatched—pink and yellow, smiley faces drawn on
each one in black marker. The desk is covered in torn
wrapping paper. A cake sits in the center, lopsided, its
frosting cracked. A single candle flickers, already half-
melted.

The speaker clicks on.

"Happy birthday, Christina."

Her voice is gleeful, like a child performing for
guests.

I don't respond. My name isn't Christina. The silence stretches.

"Did you forget?" she sings. "It's your big day. Come on, don't be rude."

I force myself to stand. My legs are stiff from yesterday's smiling game. The marker lines are still faintly smeared across my face. I shuffle forward and stare at the cake.

Written in shaky red icing: WELCOME HOME, CHRISTINA.

"Say it," she demands softly.

I swallow hard. My throat is dry. I hate this game. I hate it more than all the others.

"…Thank you, Alice."

A sigh of satisfaction.

"Good girl."

The music fades. I notice the gifts now. Three boxes, wrapped in familiar paper—*my paper*. The kind I used last year, hidden in the back closet. Silver with tiny stars. My stomach lurches.

"These are for you," she says sweetly. "Things I picked out myself. Thought they might bring back memories."

I reach for the first box with shaking hands. I tear the paper slowly.

Inside:

My old bracelet. The one I thought months ago. A simple chain with a tiny charm—two interlocked stars. I used to wear it every day. I hold it like it's burning me.

"Do you like it?" she asks. "You left it behind, Christina. I'm just giving it back."

I don't speak. I move to the second box. It's heavier. I open it. Inside: *A photo frame.* My photo frame.

The one from my nightstand. Only now the photo inside isn't what it was. It's been changed. It used to be a picture of me and my parents at graduation.

Now, it's me, standing alone. My face is scratched out with red ink. A smiley face drawn in its place.

I drop it. It shatters.

"Oops," she says.

The last box waits for me. Smaller than the others. I don't want to open it. But I do.

Inside: *A note.* Folded neatly.

I recognize the paper instantly—cream-colored, gold-edged. Cassie used to use stationery like this when we were kids.

I unfold it.

Dear Alice,

I'm sorry I couldn't be there today. But I'm so proud of you.
I love you. Always.

- B.

I stare at the signature. *Bridgette.* But this isn't real. This can't be real. My hands start to shake. I can't breathe.

"You don't remember that one?" she asks softly. "I found it in your attic. You saved everything, didn't you? You used to read it at night, over and over. Thought maybe you'd forgotten."

I crumple the note in my fist.

"Why are you doing this?" I choke. "Why would you—"

"Because you're me now, Christina." Her voice is bright, almost happy. "And I want you to remember what it feels like to lose everything. That's how you start over. That's how I did it."

She pauses.

"Besides, what's a birthday without gifts?"

The candle flickers again.

I stare at it. At the wreckage of the photo. At the bracelet I thought I'd lost in another life.

Tears burn at the corners of my eyes, but I don't let them fall.

She wants me to cry. She wants me to break.

So I don't.

I pick up the knife meant for the cake and drive it straight through the frosting, down to the table. I drag it across, slicing the words in half.

There's silence.

Then a low chuckle through the speaker.

"…Well. You're not as soft as I thought."

I turn toward the ceiling.

"Happy birthday, Alice."

The speaker cuts out.

And the candle finally dies.

A second later, the red timer above the door flickers to life: **01:00:00** It begins to count down.

Chris's voice crackles back in—light and sing-song again.

"One hour, Christina. Play with your new toys, eat some cake. After that… bedtime meds. Don't make me come down there."

Clunk.

The chute opens. The same black case. I don't even flinch.

Inside: The syringe. The vial. The note.

Smile big. Sleep deep. I'll be watching.

The timer ticks on above me, like a bomb strapped to the wall.

I sit beside the ruined cake. The broken frame. The smiley balloons bobbing on strings.

I don't touch the toys. I don't touch the cake. I just watch the seconds burn down, knowing exactly how this ends.

FORTY EIGHT

There's something playing.

Low at first. Like a whisper through the vents.

I sit up on the mattress, my mouth dry, the frosting still clinging to my fingertips. I hadn't eaten the cake, not really. Just touched it. Smeared it across the desk until the smiley face started to melt.

The voice grows louder.

Not Chris. A man.

"You said you'd come back."

Pause. A shaky breath.

"I waited. I waited every day and you never came."

Click.

A new voice now—this time a woman. Tight, furious. "Don't act like you didn't know. You let it happen. You stood there and you let it happen."

Click.

A child crying. Distant, muffled, like it's been shoved inside a box.

Then Chris. Her voice slides in like a knife behind my ear. Soft. Mocking.

"Let's play another game."

I don't move. I don't speak.

"You've heard them now," she continues. "Three voices. Three stories. Three different monsters."

Silence.

Then: "Pick one."

I blink.

"What?"

"Pick the monster, Alice. Who deserves to be locked away forever? Who would you throw in the dark and leave to rot?"

More silence. The kind that hums like electricity under my skin.

"I—" My voice cracks. "What are you talking about?"

She clicks her tongue. "You need to learn how to choose. You never were very good at that."

Another click. The woman's voice again.

"I begged you," she sobs. "I begged you to help me."

Chris again, louder now. Almost cheerful.

"They're all telling the truth. And they're all lying. That's what makes this fun."

I stand, fists clenched. "Why are you doing this?"

A long breath. Then, softly: "Because I want you to see what I see."

The speaker goes quiet. But the timer lights up on the wall again.

00:59:59

I already know what it means. I glance at the needle on the tray. Chris doesn't say it this time. She doesn't have to.

I press my hands over my ears, but it doesn't matter. The recordings start again.

"You said you'd come back."

"I waited. I waited every day and you never came."

Click.

"Don't act like you didn't know. You let it happen. You stood there and you let it happen."

Click.

Crying. A child again. The same sound warped now. Slower. Wet.

Click.

"You said you'd come back…"

The timer flashes on the wall.

00:42:18

I spin around the room, searching for something—anything. The speaker. The wires. A way to rip it out. But there's nothing. It's all buried in concrete and steel.

"Matt?" I whisper. "Is that Matt's voice? Is that his mother?"

No answer. Just another round.

"You let it happen—"

"You never came—"

The child's sobbing, rising now into a shriek.

00:32:03

I pace. I mutter names under my breath like a prayer I barely believe in. *Matt. His father. My father. Bridgette's dad. Hers. Mine.*

"Please stop," I whisper.

It keeps playing.

"You never came—"

"You let it happen—"

Screaming.

00:19:51

I scream back. "WHAT DO YOU WANT FROM ME?!" Nothing. Except the voices.

"You said you'd come back…"

They loop again.

00:12:40

"Pick one," Chris had said. Pick the monster. Pick the one who deserves the dark.

I back into the corner and cover my ears tighter. It's like they're inside me now—bouncing around the inside of my skull, turning bone to static.

"You never came—"

"You let it happen—"

"You never—"

"You let—"

00:05:03

My whole body shakes.

00:02:49

I scream until my throat tears.

00:01:16

Then—

"CHRISTINA, STOP!"

Silence.

The timer freezes.

The light cuts out.

Dark.

Dark so heavy it's a weight on my chest. No buzz. No voice. No screaming. Even my own breath feels like an intrusion.

Oh no, I messed up.

Click.

The speaker flares back to life. A whisper.

"That's *not* my name."

And from the shadows behind the wall, *clunk.* The syringe tray unlocks. The light over it blinks on. Just that one.

Dim. Pale blue. Cold.

I don't move.

But I will.

I always do.

FORTY NINE

It starts with light.

Not the cold kind from the timer, or the buzzing fluorescents above my cot.

This light is warm. Yellow. Flickering.

Like candlelight.

I'm standing in a hallway. No... not standing. Floating. My feet don't make noise on the wood floor.

There's something soft in my hand.

A doll. Its button eye dangles from a thread.

The hallway stretches ahead—lined with doors. Every door has a smiley face carved into it.

They smile with teeth.

I try to turn around, but I don't have a body.

I don't feel fear, not yet. Just confusion, like I've dropped something important but can't remember what it was.

The first door opens.

Bridgette.

She's sitting cross-legged on her pink carpet, braiding Cassie's hair. Cassie's face is wrong, though—blank, too smooth, like her features were erased.

Bridgette doesn't notice. She just keeps braiding, whispering something under her breath.

I lean in.

She's saying, "You have to keep a smile on. You have to keep a smile on. You have to keep—"

Click.

The second door.

Matt. Tied to a chair. His mouth taped shut. His eyes swollen shut.

Behind him, a woman whispers through the dark.

"Don't make me do it again. I told you to behave."

She's smiling too.

They all are.

Click.

The hallway warps sideways. I stumble forward—no, fall—through the third door.

It slams shut behind me.

I'm in a mirror maze.

Every reflection is me.

But not me now. Me as a child. Me covered in blood. Me smiling like Chris.

I open my mouth to scream, but the reflections beat me to it.

"You said you'd come back."

"You let it happen."

"You left us."

"You left me."

Their mouths stretch wide until they crack.

I press my hands to my face. But the hands aren't mine. They're thin. Pale. The nails are painted pink. There's a scar on the left wrist.

I spin toward the nearest mirror—

Chris stares back at me.

Not smiling.

Just watching.

And I hear her voice, deep inside my chest now, not from the speaker:

"Good girl. You're getting it."

***

I wake up.

Blinking. Gasping for air. Drenched in sweat.

The light's too clean. White. Sharp. Still.

The walls are tiled. One-way mirror in front of me.
A table. Two metal chairs. Interrogation room. There's
a file folder on the desk. Thick. Heavy. My name is
written on it. But it's crossed out.

Above it, in neat block letters:

CHRISTINA WARD

My heart skips.

The chair across from me is empty. The one behind
me isn't.

Chris doesn't speak. Not yet. She just breathes. I
can feel it, like heat on the back of my neck. I reach out
to open the file, but she finally speaks.

"Christina," she says, casual.

And I answer.

"Yeah?"

The word is out before I can catch it. My blood
goes cold. I didn't mean it. I didn't *think*. I just…
responded. Like it really was my name.

Silence stretches thin and wide around us. Inside, something twists. A little voice that sounds like mine whispers:

She's getting into your head.

She's turning the game into reality.

I stare at the file again. No more hesitation. It's time to turn the page.

FIFTY

I sit in the interrogation room long after Chris is gone.

The folder's still open in front of me.

Inside: pages of fake records. School transcripts I never had. Psychological profiles. Disciplinary reports with my name—no, her name—stamped in red across the top.

CHRISTINA WARD

DOB: blank.

Diagnosis: Unstable. Compliant when medicated. Dangerous when not.

I flip to the next page.

A photo of me. Recent. Too recent.

I'm wearing her clothes. Staring blankly at the camera like I don't know who I am.

I shut the file. Slowly. Quietly.

She wants me to panic.

She wants me to scream.

She wants me to lose track of where Alice ends and Christina begins.

I won't give her the satisfaction. Not anymore. I scan the room for cameras. Obvious ones. Hidden ones. Doesn't matter. I look anyway.

Then I lean forward and rest my chin on my hands like I'm tired. Like I've given up. I count to sixty.

Once.

Twice.

Three times.

Then I let my eyes drift to the floor vent near the corner.

Small. Narrow.

But maybe not too small.

Chris never let me see the layout of this place. But if there's ventilation, there's another room. Another way in. Or out.

I tuck that thought away. Wrap it in steel.

The door clicks open.

She steps inside with two cups of tea. Like we're old friends on a porch somewhere.

Her smile is soft. Almost maternal.

"I brought peppermint," she says. "I know it helps with your nerves."

Your.

Not *my*.

I nod. I take the cup. I don't drink.

"Thanks," I say, even though my stomach twists.

She sits across from me. Folds her hands neatly on the table.

"You've been doing so well."

I stare at her.

"I have?"

She tilts her head. "You're adjusting. Letting go. That's important."

I nod again. Smile, even. Let her think I'm folding. Let her think she's winning.

Later, when she leaves, I slide a spoon under the table. Tuck it into the waistband of the skirt she gave me. Perfect if sharpened.

I press my palm to the edge and feel it bite.

Not enough to cut.

But enough to remind me:

I'm still here.

And I'm not going to die down here.

Not like her.

Not like him.

Not like the others.

I spend the rest of the hour pacing the perimeter of the room.

To her, I probably look nervous.

Good. Let her think that.

But I'm counting vents. Watching how long the lights take to dim when she closes the door. Timing the hum between speaker clicks. Noting the screws in the floor panels. The shape of the camera eye.

I press my fingers into the edge of the mirror. Tap each corner.

If I'm going to get out, I need to know everything.

Patterns.

Gaps.

Weak spots.

Maybe that means faking another breakdown. Maybe it means earning her trust. Maybe it means smiling so wide she forgets I still have teeth.

Tomorrow, I'll test the door after she leaves. Maybe it'll be locked. Maybe not.

If it's not—then I'll know something.

If it is—then I'll learn something else.

Every answer is a breadcrumb. And I'm done starving.

I don't need hope. I need leverage. And now I know where to look.

FIFTY ONE

I wake up with a plan.

It's not rage anymore. Not fear.

It's precision.

I've played this moment over in my mind so many times, it feels like it already happened. Every glance. Every word. Every false move she might make. I've memorized her routines like scripture.

The spoon stays tucked in the pillow, but I haven't touched it in days. It was never about stabbing her. I know my body too well—I know what happens when I see blood.

Even a drop and I'm out. And she? She doesn't bleed quietly.

So I found another way.

The lights flicker on early again. Like last time. A pattern.

She's coming.

I sit up, smooth the blanket over my lap, and pull Matt's jacket tight around me. I position myself in the corner. Back straight. Calm. Controlled.

The door clicks.

I don't flinch.

Chris walks in holding a tray. Probably oatmeal again—warm, sweet-smelling, like comfort you didn't ask for.

"Good morning," she says, all honey and delusion. "You're glowing today. I think this place suits you."

I give her a soft smile. Measured. Small. Let her see what she wants to see.

"I've been thinking," she says, setting the tray down. "You've come so far. Maybe it's time you earned a little fresh air."

I freeze—just for a breath. Then: "Outside?"

She nods. "Just a trial run. A few minutes. But I think you're ready."

She turns toward the door.

Doesn't close it all the way.

Leaves it cracked.

A test.

Perfect.

I wait.

I count thirty seconds. Long enough for her footsteps to fade, but not long enough for the cameras to catch hesitation.

I move. Not loud. Not fast.

I slide the pillow open and pull the spoon free—not to stab. Just to carry.

Then I move to the grate I've been watching for over a week. Lower left wall. Behind the desk. Covered in dust and spiderwebs. It's held in by four screws.

Three are already loose.

One more twist.

One more breath.

And it pops free.

I crawl inside.

It's tighter than I expected. My shoulders scrape both sides. The metal groans. Dust clings to my mouth, my nose, my throat. My lungs scream, but I keep moving.

She said she wanted me to have air.

Fine.

Let her choke on the irony.

I follow the main shaft—left, then down. I mapped it in my mind after every forced shower, every cleaning cycle. The system loops. But one junction curves sharply toward cooler air.

I take it.

It's narrow—too narrow. But I force myself through. Elbows drag. Knees burn. My fingers bleed on the rusted seams, but I bite down and keep crawling.

Then I hear it.

A faint sound at first.

My name.

"Alice... Alice..."

The voice stretches out, warped and distant. A cruel echo bouncing off metal walls.

Chris.

Her voice is soft, syrupy, mocking.

"You can't run. You're mine. You'll always be mine."

I press forward, heart pounding. The walls close in, my breath shallow. I shake off the voice like poison.

No.

Not anymore.

Then: light.

A sliver.

A small square of sun slashing across the dust. I slam my foot once—twice—into the grate. It groans.

The third kick knocks it loose.

The world spills open around me. I tumble into grass. Real grass.

Wet with dew. Cold on my bare arms. Sun on my face. Wind across my skin. I gasp and crawl forward until I can stand.

I spin, breath ragged, vision flickering.

Behind me, a rusted vent rises from the ground—hidden beneath ivy and weeds. Just another pipe, another scar on the land.

I shove the grate back into place and collapse beside it.

My lungs burn. My body shakes. My knuckles drip.

But I'm out. Really out.

Standing in a field of wildflowers, alone, alive, and finally free.

FIFTY TWO

My head whips around so fast I nearly collapse from dizziness. I have no idea where I am or what direction to go, but standing here frozen in this damp field of daisies is not an option. My legs scream at me to run.

Breathe.

Chris is down there. Still alive. Still capable. And if I don't move now, she'll drag me right back into that concrete grave and seal it shut for good.

Breathe!

A groan echoes up from the open bunker hatch. I don't stop to listen—I sprint. The sun breaks through the trees behind me, a blinding, brilliant gold that warms my back like a silent cheerleader urging me forward.

Left. Right. Left. Right.

The wet grass slaps at my ankles as I push through the field. My feet are numb from cold and raw from days barefoot, but I don't care. Every second counts.

"**GET BACK HERE!!**" Her scream rips through the morning air.

She's close.

I don't dare turn around. If I see her face—if I see the rage in her eyes—I'll freeze. I know I will.

She always said I was good at her game. That I could keep up.

Let's see how she likes it when I win.

The trees close in like jagged teeth through the fog. I push into the woods, ducking under branches, scraping my arms and legs without even feeling the pain. Leaves and limbs blur past me. I don't stop. I won't stop.

Don't look back. Don't stop. Just run.

A rock thuds into a tree beside me. She's throwing things.

Another hits the ground near my heel. Then one grazes my shoulder. I stumble, but keep moving, gasping for air, throat burning.

And then—impact. A rock slams into my lower back.

Pain explodes through my spine, but I don't slow down. Blood is seeping down my waistband, but I force my body to keep running, faster, harder. I force my brain past it's limits. Don't focus on the blood.

"STOP RUNNING!" Her voice cracks behind me. She's getting tired. Good.

The forest thins. Light. I can see light.

Please be a road. Please be a road.

I taste blood—I've been clenching my jaw so tightly my lip split open. I try to loosen it. Try to focus.

But the ground gives out beneath me.

I tumble—over branches, roots, stones—smashing into everything on the way down. The world spins and spins until it spits me out at the bottom of the hill.

Everything hurts. My limbs are scratched and bruised and bleeding. My head is pounding. But I can move. I'm still alive.

GET UP.

I crawl to my knees, dizzy, panting. And then I hear it—movement above.

Chris.

She's at the top of the hill, scanning for me.

Her eyes lock onto mine.

No more mask. No more smile.

Just pure, seething rage.

I snatch up a rock. It's not much, but it's something.

She starts to slide down the hill after me.

I run.

Every nerve in my body is on fire. I don't even feel like I'm inside my skin anymore—I'm just instinct. Fear. Willpower.

And then I hear it.

A car.

I push myself even more.

Through the pain and through the blood trying to knock me on my ass.

I push through years of trauma and heart break.

Through days of stress and lack of sleep.

I push.

For Matt. For my mom. For myself.

A road.

Black asphalt cutting through the trees like a lifeline. My bare feet slap down onto it and I nearly collapse from the shock of it.

But I keep running.

No cars. No houses. Just this road and the open world it connects to.

I glance behind me—just once.

Chris is crashing through the undergrowth behind me, feral, wild, still chasing.

I face forward.

And I run.

I run and I don't look back.

SEE YOU SOON